I0611287

SURVIVAL OF A SPECIES

PART ONE

THE A-MORTAL GENE

BY

COLIN SETTERFIELD

Paperback Book Edition
Copyright © 2016 Colin Setterfield
ALL RIGHTS RESERVED

ISBN-978-988719-06-1

TABLE OF CONTENTS

PROLOGUE

I thought the A-Mortal Gene through longevity, would ensure humankind's quality of life and ultimate survival, however, there are too many variables in our universe. We plan and we execute—to be hijacked by an infinite set of probabilities, which take over the course of life and death....

But I should not get ahead of myself—.

∞∞

One

A Rude Wake-up Call

0630 hours, 24th June, 2315 C.E.

At first the sound crept through my subconscious, like an angry beetle caught inside a metal container.

The noise continued with greater intensity and destroyed any hope of further slumber. I sat up in the bed and struck my head on the overhead canopy of the pod with some force. The angry beetle turned out to be the emergency buzzer—not the sound of the usual wakeup call, but rather a noisy screech. I knew it spelled trouble.

Every spacer aboard the Andromeda hated to hear this sound. Worse still, it wasn't general quarters, but a summons from the bridge—an urgent call from my Uncle Sid. I canceled the alarm.

"President Commander?"

The voice of my uncle boomed through the speaker. "Beckett, see me in my office, immediately!"

My uncle, Sid Conroy, President Commander and owner of the space-mining vessel Andromeda, never appeared to sleep. This is the general perception of the space craft personnel—I have the privilege, or curse, to be his nephew and the one person he picks on the most. The Andromeda is as large as a city and boasts a population of five thousand people, all of whom work for the Galactic Mineral Mining Corporation and one of fifteen mining ventures in the asteroid belt.

Over a period pf fifteen years, Uncle Sid built the enterprise into the largest mining operation of its sort in the galaxy—well, that's what we believed, anyway.

The Andromeda's mining activities took place on the edge of the asteroid belt, a mineral treasure trove about ten million kilometers beyond Mars.

Unlike the tenuous relationship with my father, the bond between my uncle and I stood strong, the evident legacy of Dad's absenteeism.

He enjoyed the position of chief bio-molecular geneticist for the New World Earth Genetic Foundation, a time-consuming post. This turned him into a work-focused father, never around when needed.

Dad's affluent financial credit provided for my physical and educational needs but because of his un-availability, any comfort and advice always came from Uncle Sid. Despite many months of the year spent on the Andromeda, Sid Conroy always gave me his attention. Up to the time I joined the crew, our communication happened via holographic exchange.

With reference to education, dad financed my passage through the New World Earth Institute for Higher Learning, but   Uncle Sid guided me through the problems of life. Dad paid for my special education and provided me with an advantage, which resulted in one major drawback—the direction of study had to be his choice, not mine—his way or the highway.

Because of its unique method of education, the New World Earth Institute of Learning created the image of high education for the wealthy. No lecturers, classrooms, or student body dignified the campus. It resembled a neuroscience clinic—the application of POMI reinforcement, the very latest approach, replaced all traditional methods of education. POMI stands for Passive Osmotic Memory Induction, a step above the old university hands-on education experience.

Incumbents linked to a Sensory Stimulus Inductor, which introduced knowledge into the memory banks at a much higher rate than the standard, human learning process. It took four intensive weeks for me to receive four years of material and instruction, a further two weeks of tests to make sure the information settled into the memory—a weird experience, overall.

The result: I qualified as a bio-molecular geneticist, Level Four, with no ambition for the field and even less interest in the subject.

When I left the institute to hit the streets and live like a bum, the shit hit the fan with my dad, but Uncle Sid understood my reasons. After Dad cut me off financially my uncle offered much needed financial relief, but pride would not allow me to accept. It dawned on me—after almost twelve years of tending bars and part-time work in minimum credit positions, all to support my ambition to become a pro surfer, there needed to be some major adjustments made. At the age of thirty-two my life showed no progress or promise, but desperate to deny my father the satisfaction of a dutiful son who followed in his footsteps, I eschewed the temptation to involve myself in genetic engineering. For a while I indulged my infantile pride until Uncle Sid came to my rescue and I accepted his offer to join the venture in the asteroid belt. He lured me into the world of Quantum Instrument Technology, a professional pursuit which held some interest for me. Sid Conroy, never married and remained a bachelor all his life, the reason for which I would later understand with greater clarity. With no children of his own he treated me like a son, an indulgence which annoyed my father beyond words.

I left my cubicle and stepped into the verticap to be transported upward, toward the bridge. The sheer size of the Andromeda often caused newbies to lose their way in the maze of corridors, however, a three-month probationary period helped me gain a knowledge of the craft's complex layout.

There appeared to be no problem with the Bridge instrumentation—the most probable reason for my uncle's call. My job entailed flight equipment maintenance, the best area for my induction as a trainee and further promotion, to become the eventual owner of the corporation.

I stopped at the entrance to the office of the PC's personal assistant, Freda Banning, and asked, "Do you always start work this early?"

She looked up at me and smiled. "Some-times—go through, Beckett, he's waiting for you."

Sid Conroy sat at his desk, engrossed with a report on the holographic viewer. He continued to read while I stood at attention and waited. We always observed flight etiquette when on the bridge or in the presence of staff members, in order to respect the fundamentals of spacer protocol.

The president commander looked up from the report. His hand moved toward the control panel in front of him to activate the entrance force field—it appeared this was to be a private talk—all the bridge sounds disappeared. I stared straight ahead and pondered my fate.

"At ease, Beckett," the PC stated.

He spoke with a relaxed tone and I flopped into one of the chairs adjacent to the large, polished oak desk, with relief. Real wood is extremely hard to come by but my uncle often collected rare oddities.

"I'm afraid I have some very bad news for the both of us," he said.

"How so?" I asked. The PC's words raised my level of alertness.

He dropped his chin. "There's no way to soften this blow. Your father..." he hesitated, displaying a rare moment of emotion, "...is dead."

∞∞

TWO

Bad News

I half rose out of my seat, to stare at him.

The president commander shifted in his seat. "My brother...your father....was killed in an accident yesterday."

I sank back into the chair. All I could manage was an inadequate stammer. "But how—where?"

Sid Conroy, always a very pragmatic person, rarely showed any outward signs of emotion, but I saw the signs of moisture in his eyes as he stared into the viewer on his desktop.

"No one seems to know the exact details, but it's thought he had been electrocuted while working on a special project."

My eyes must have glazed over because my uncle reached over the desktop to clutch my wrist. I felt numbed to the bone.

Uncle Sid let go of my wrist and leaned back in his chair and the worry lines asserted themselves around his eyes.

"I completely understand this must come as a terrible shock to you—it's probably best you take some time alone in your cubicle—try to come to grips with the status quo. We can talk later. I need to rearrange my schedule and decide what to do next."

I nodded and stood, but felt no real symptoms of grief or regret. "Thanks, Uncle Sid—I'll do that."

I turned on my heel and strode out of his office, with every intention to go to my cubicle, but a more original thought crossed my mind; I headed for the Liquid Star, a bar I often frequented when off shift—seemed like the best place to regain my composure.

The emptiness of the bar didn't surprise me as the regular shift change-over would still be another hour.

The computer took my order, a double whiskey on the rocks, as I placed my hand on the credit scanner to show my available credits.

Everyone received a very limited allowance for the purchase of alcohol. A good reason, like a birthday party, would be needed to obtain any extra privilege.

I hated the system of control we lived under but the realities of human nature and system abuse made it necessary. No tendencies for overindulgence could be tolerated on the Andromeda—too risky. Many lives depended on the sober vigil of every spacer—everyone performed important functions and, if neglected, the safety of the entire ship could be jeopardized.

The computer spoke with a stiff formality.

'Ensign Beckett Conroy, GMMC 156901; the record shows you should be starting your shift within two hours. Consumption of alcohol at this time is not permitted.'

It made no sense to argue with the computer—the stupid programs prompted standard answers with no thought for reason—Yes and no, black and white—the way it worked in space. I longed for the freedom of my old beach-patrol days when my time was my own. Too much change over the years made my former pursuit less attractive. Certain, very pertinent facts, jeered at me; for one, overcrowded in-city beaches no longer provided adequate relaxation. Second: the dramatic rise in costs to gain use of the facilities made them almost prohibitive.

Synthetic beaches, situated within the domed configuration of smaller cities did not take up an abundance of space. Quantum City, however, could not be accommodated within the limits of the main dome, which increased the costs beyond my financial abilities.

For the past hundred years, due to the high radiation factor of the Earth's atmosphere, natural beaches ceased to be a viable pursuit. With in-city beaches, time allocations for the smallest patch of synthetic sand could be procured by the purchase of an annual membership—at a phenomenal cost. The wave-pool also, at all times, remained packed with people and much to the pool management's chagrin, complaints about wide variations in temperature requirements, remained a thorny issue with everyone.

My claim to fame rested on several small trophies, won in various surfing competitions but the cash prizes provided no more than beer-money.

I dispelled the negative thoughts and moved out of the bar with full intentions of making a return to my cubicle. Someone else, however, anticipated my sudden need for alcoholic distraction.

"I thought you might be here," she said.

I stopped dead in my tracks and turned— Uncle Sid's personal assistant to the rescue.

"Freda, what brings you down here at this time?" I asked.

Trust her to show at the very moment I needed my space.

"Sid told me about your dad—I feel so bad for the both of you—what an awful thing to happen," she replied. "I thought you might need some company and I knew you might try the Liquid Star. The computer wouldn't sell you any liquor, right?"

I hoped she would not offer to hold my hand for the rest of the day. I wanted to be alone and needed a drink—not a shoulder to cry on.

"I have a bottle of Supernova in my cubicle, if you're interested. I'm sure it'll help settle things in your head."

Freda's a whiz with technology and a paragon of organizational ability. My uncle often said he would be incapacitated in many aspects of his command without her.

She possessed a heart of gold and would do all within her power to be helpful, if she thought you needed it. Tender-hearted, she'd share her thoughts freely but all too often, good virtue is countered by a negative side—she suffered from a bipolar disorder, the dramatic highs and lows of which, at inconvenient times, could change her demeanor in a moment.

Despite the medical prowess of the ages, a complete cure for this disorder still eluded the medical field. The ability to modify DNA to reduce anomalies often caused the production of anti-bodies, which produced a bounce-back effect, to disturb the modification.

At least a much more effective medication evolved over time, to stabilize the disorder. Freda's main problem did not lie with the disorder itself but a resistance to use of the medication.

The bottle of Supernova got my attention—good whiskey and expensive, too.

"I could do with a stiff drink—but just one, then I should get back to my cubicle."

She nodded, grabbed my arm and propelled me toward the verticap. I liked Freda but she wasn't my type—not that women fell over me for attention, but I always took care in the choice of my dates, to avoid any serious commitments.

She caste me a sideways glance. "We probably shouldn't be drinking alcohol at this time of the morning, but what the heck—it's the best thing for shock, so I'm told."

My intuition suggested Freda might be a little more than infatuated with me. Whenever I visited the president commander, she emanated an unmistakable atmosphere of silent appraisal. Not a great deal of dialogue passed between us but I became sensitive to the flirtatious vibe.

After arrival at Freda's cubicle, we entered and she positioned me on the sofa, then slipped into the small kitchenette. The brief respite gave me the opportunity to focus on the situation at hand. My father had died, and I didn't know how I felt about it.

Maybe the cause of my ambivalence was due to delayed shock but I thought of his life-long absenteeism—not a coldness, but de facto disinterest. I vowed if fatherhood arose in the vague and uncertain future, my children would never suffer the same fate as I. They would never be treated with such disdain.

Freda returned with two glasses in one hand and the bottle of Supernova in the other. "How do you like it?"

"On the rocks, and make it a double."

I noticed the sensuous appeal of her lips, which revealed the symmetrical, uniform white teeth, as she concentrated on pouring the drinks.

She dispensed the Supernova with a heavy hand, for which I was thankful and sat on the couch beside me. We sipped for about twenty seconds before she spoke again.

"Let's talk about your father."

"With all due respect, there isn't really anything I want to discuss right now."

She ogled me with her large sapphire-blue eyes and smiled. "I think you might, after what I'm about to tell you."

I was intrigued. Then she dropped the bombshell.

"Your dad's death was not an accident."

∞∞

Three

Not My Finest Performance

I believe Freda's desire to startle me out of my indifference, resulted in a marginal effect toward a reaction of alarm. The Supernova in competition with mental acuity caused my response to fall short of the expected astonishment.

"Not an accident?"

"Yes. Sid wanted to tell you, but thought you might need a little damage control before hearing the truth. Your dad's death happened under very suspicious circumstances."

The words percolated through my thoughts as Freda took another sip of her drink. She assumed my silence to be a consent for continuance and launched into details about the initial investigation by the Quantum City police.

"Your father was working on a very secret project to do with human longevity. It would appear he discovered something very significant. His secretary, Carla Jensen, typed up a summary of all the experiments as he went along, but the results of the final week were not passed on to her. There's strong indication he was nearing a break-through and then...," tears welled up in her eyes as she gathered her thoughts.

"I met your father about ten years ago. I found him approachable and so good-looking and his natural charm always put me at ease. Although he knew so much more than I, about genetics, Padraig always made me feel important."

After a pause to regain more of her compo-sure she continued the brief. "He left you a mes-sage. This is weird, but it's as though he knew his life was in danger. The prevailing circumstances at the time of his accident appear a little improbable but the police cannot fully determine it to be foul play."

"What message did he leave?" My throat became dry.

"It's best you hear it from Sid. He'll proba-bly be mad at me—that I've told you, I mean."

With gradual consideration and the onslaught of shock I responded to the news of my father's death. To say I felt grief would be dishonest. More like remorse; I hadn't spoken to him for three months—my mind flashed back to our last conversation—an argument. An opportunity for a geneticist arose at the Genetic Foundation where he worked, and he begged me to take it.

The position would have paid well and certainly kick-started my career in bio-genetics but the thought of such regular and close contact with my dad did not appeal to me. My career in quantum maintenance, aboard the Andromeda, although still in its infancy, suited me fine. He appeared obsessed with the idea I should carry his research to further heights.

My reverie plunged the cubicle into an uncomfortable silence. Freda placed her hand on my arm.

"Are you okay, Beckett?"

"Yeah, sure—I was just taking a walk down memory lane."

She stared at me with sympathetic eyes but managed a weak grin.

"It's okay to show your feelings—if there's anything I can do, please don't hesitate to ask."

The offer came from genuine empathy for my situation, however, behind my remorse lurked a storm of darkness. A tempest not yet ready to be explored.

"I had better get back to my cubicle," I said.

An attempt to keep the emotion out of my voice proved difficult.

"Thanks for the drink and information."

"You're very welcome."

She wiped away a few rogue strands of loose hair. The trendy mix of jet-black and peroxide streaks gave her the appearance of a young teenage girl, but I judged her to be in the early thirties.

She activated the exit force field and I turned to leave.

"Can you get me an hour with my uncle when he's back on shift?" I asked.

"I'll do that—I'll buzz you when I know."

I thanked Freda and headed for the verti-cap. The ride took a few seconds and gave me the opportunity to view my reflection in the mirrored walls. It did not surprise me to see the reflection of a haggard face and impassive, gloomy eyes. With a sudden sadness I felt a lot older than my thirty-two years.

How much time spent on the bum, around in-city beaches? How much financial loss through low-hour shifts for minimum credits? It all seemed so infantile ——the pursuit of some non-descript trophy and consequent struggle to keep my head above water. A rush of emotion overcame me and my eyes misted up. I bowed my head for a moment but an alarm brought me back to the moment—my floor level.

The force field retracted and gave access onto the platform but I stood unable to move, with my mind in turmoil, locked into the past and paralyzed by fear of the status quo. The force field re-engaged and the verticap moved toward another level. I lunged at the mirror to pound the reflection of my own imbecilic image.

"Fucking idiot! All these wasted years and what have you achieved? Nothing—absolutely nothing!"

In silence, the reflection stared back at me and it shocked me to see the tears—maybe deep inside a human being existed after all.

Ten minutes later, back in my cubicle, the ablution-chamber made a wonderful difference to the way I felt. The warm, watery mist felt pleasurable against the contours of my body as it cleaned off the night's grime.

The driers activated and within thirty seconds and I exited the booth to step into the nano-auto-dress fabricator. Selection of the standard spacer-suit from the holographic screen above my head followed and I placed my arms out in front of me. The device spun a thin nano-robotic fiber around my body, which formed into the shape of my dress requirement.

I pushed a button on the wall and ordered breakfast from the meal-replicator and—took a minute for the production of my choice.

My mind still stewed over the bad news. An emotion presented itself which caused me to drum my fingers un-rhythmically on the countertop—Dad's sudden death left me mystified and angry.

Like my mother's departure so many years before—no goodbye and no closure.

It would be sometime before this state of mental anguish settled to allow me organized thought along more rational lines. With breakfast over, the sleeping-pod beckoned. A short rest would be good—help me deal with the effects of the whiskey and tension. Hours later it happened all over again. That confounded emergency buzzer—damn. I wanted to smash it to pieces.

∞∞

Four

Confrontation with the President Commander

I rubbed sleep from my eyes as the memory of my early-morning conversation with Freda returned.

"Hi—I'm awake."

"Your uncle will see you in five."

"I'll come up immediately."

The chrono on the wall read 1100 hours. The need to find out what happened to my father now became a priority. Was it murder, or did my father mislead everyone and commit suicide? Maybe he followed the same path as my mother—was I perhaps a contributor to their deaths? Questions flooded my mind like a torrential downpour.

The verticap shot straight up to the bridge without a stop and within a short space of time I stood at Freda's office entrance. Uncle Sid's office led off hers and I knew she disliked anyone to pass straight through without a short conference—she maintained a fierce protection of him and an admirable passion for her responsibilities.

She glanced up and smiled. "You can go straight in, Beckett. He's waiting."

I dispensed with the usual protocol and moved straight to one of the chairs perched in front of the desk, where I sat to wait for his attention. Should I be angry with regard to his previous omission of the details?

In consideration, I could, perhaps understand the oversight—he feared an adverse reaction from me. I guess I can live with that. It seemed childish and inconsiderate to hold him responsible for such a minor infringement.

Sid looked up and held my gaze a few seconds. He leaned back in the large, executive chair and spoke with a quiet tone.

"Beckett—I'm sorry I didn't tell you immediately about our suspicions. Perhaps I should have been a little more forthcoming, but it's out now. Freda should have conferred with me before telling you."

"Let's forget it—Freda said there was a message dad left me."

Uncle Sid gathered himself and looked through the open door at Freda. "Get in here, Freda—you're pretty much a part of this anyway." She shot out of her chair and moved into the office. He activated the force field at the entrance to separate us from the rest of the bridge and my pulse quickened; I needed to hear about my father's final wishes for me—I thought I knew—nothing different from what he always wanted.

Freda sat in the chair alongside mine and regarded me silent appraisal. This time I found it to be a comfort. I needed a friend.

The president commander hesitated for a moment to consolidate his thoughts.

"It appeared your father suspected he was in danger. He recorded a message specifically for you, three days before he died. Seems the last of his notes were uploaded to an information-vial and hidden. It contains the final data and result of his breakthrough. Our interstellar communications group delivered the message to me during the previous shift."

My patience wore thin. "But what is the message?"

"I'm getting to that," he said quietly. "Your father was anxious for you to know he finally came to terms with your decision not to follow in his footsteps. He applauded you for having your own mind and pursuing your own interests."

I flinched slightly and Freda, bless her heart, reached over to place a hand of reassurance on my arm.

Uncle Sid continued. "Your dad loved you very much."

I leaned back in the chair and looked at the ceiling in an attempt to conceal my frustration. Freda leaned closer and gripped my arm with a greater intensity.

"The main crux of his message, however, deals with the need for you to take up on a highly significant discovery in longevity genetics. He stresses how extremely important the break-through will be to humankind. Unfortunately, it seems an outside agency had become informed about the significance of the work which forced him to work on it in secret."

I rediscovered my voice. "You mean he suspected the WGF and his own colleagues?"

"Yes—at least that's what we think. He made it clear someone was out to steal the information. As to its whereabouts, no one knows, but he left a clue you might be able to decipher. I can't make heads or tails of it, but you might—it has to be something you and he shared when you were young."

An annoyance gripped me as I thought of the implications of my dad's actions. He always wanted me to take up the cudgel and for a brief moment, a flash of the old anger arose—his conspiracy to lock me into his world. The earlier words in the message: 'having come to terms with the situation and applauding me for having my own mind,' was all bullshit.

"I don't want to hear any more!"

My words carried more venom than intended. Freda slid her hand off my arm and raised plucked eyebrows. Uncle Sid held my stare.

"It's not what you think, Beckett. Your dad trusted you implicitly. This breakthrough he talked about is obviously a very big deal. Why else would someone murder him to steal it?"

I looked at my folded hands and felt a twitch in my left eyebrow. This happened when I fell into deep conflict with myself. Freda remained silent. I wriggled around in my trussed-up thoughts but could make little sense of the situation—all I could come up with was my father's conspiratorial effort. "I don't want anything to do with it!"

Uncle Sid stood and placed his hands on the desktop; his eyes betrayed the pent up anger.

"You may have lost a father, but don't forget I have lost someone too—my brother! I want to know who is responsible for this terrible deed—even if you don't give a shit. We are taking the Excalibur to Earth to bury him and that's an order, Ensign Conroy. Is that understood?"

His words stung like micro-meteors, and I was taken aback.

"Yes, President Commander." I stood.

"Be ready to leave at 2000 hours, Ensign. I expect you at the spaceport platform, ready to travel."

I saluted, the raise of a fist to the heart and turned on my heel to leave without a backward glance. I felt Freda's sympathetic gaze follow in my wake—I wanted to bury myself.

∞∞

Five

Back to the Unfamiliar

Irritated by the sudden nature of our departure, I packed personal necessities and made my way to the spaceport. An empty passenger lounge greeted me but it came as no surprise—aboard the unscheduled flight, apart from the crew, would be Uncle Sid and I.

I peered through the large viewport at the space-dock and saw tiny wisps of cryogenic vapor escaping Excalibur's fuel transfer pipe connection.

Trussed to the giant grapple-hooks like a giant bird, the spaceship towered overhead. Beyond the confines of the lounge's window, flight-preparation engineers floated in the zero gravity to check various elements of the craft's hull.

A hand rested on my shoulder. For a brief moment, the familiar fragrance of perfume permeated the air.

"Hi, Freda. Where's Uncle Sid—what are you doing here?"

She looked at me and her eyes sparkled brightly under the lounge's overhead lights. "He's on his way. I will be coming too."

My astonishment must have showed. "Why? I thought it would only be Uncle Sid and I."

"I twisted your uncle's arm—I want to pay my respects and you'll both need someone to help finalize the arrangements."

I forced a smile. A robot space-porter wheeled in three large suitcases and dumped them onto the cargo platform to be loaded into the cargo bay. "Not traveling so light?" I joked.

"You never know what might come in handy. I only use the auto-dress for company suits. There are lots of traditionally made clothes I don't get much time to wear here on the Andromeda."

My backpack must have seemed skimpy to her. "I don't think I'll be staying too long—there's not much left for me on Earth."

Freda regarded me with sympathetic indulgence. "I think you might be surprised about your own deeper feelings once you're back there."

I didn't mean to be sarcastic but the words shot from my mouth.

"What, are you a psychiatrist now?"

She laughed. "It's not well known but I hold an advanced level-one honorarium in Industrial psychology, so—to answer your question—yes. I am well acquainted with psychiatric work."

That took the wind out of my sails. "I'm sorry, Freda. I didn't mean—"

"I understand. The five stages of grief were discovered centuries ago, but they stand as true today as they did then."

For the first time in the conversation, a genuine smile lit up on my face in remembrance of thoughts I struggled with earlier in the day.

"I recall my initial astonishment and disbelief, which after a while, transitioned into anger—I guess that's where I am at the moment."

"You've been angry for a long time, Beckett."

I was about to answer when the robotic space-porter returned with Uncle Sid in tow. One suitcase—I felt vindicated. If the president commander still held anger with regard to my recent indiscretion it didn't show. He smiled and draped his arm around my shoulders.

"Are you ready for the flight, Nephew?"

"Yes, sir, I am. It's been a while since I've traveled in space but I 'm ready."

In fact four months had elapsed since my arrival on the Andromeda. One of the most advanced spaceships ever built, Excalibur boasted some of the latest innovations in space-flight technology. Used for search and rescue, the craft found its secondary purpose as a shuttle vessel, for the ferry of Andromeda's occupants to and from our mother planet. The journey to Earth took thirty-eight hours.

A green light blinked on the entrance portal to the flight crew's entrance. A mood of quiet expectation gripped us as the captain greeted our group at the top of the walkway and then assigned travel-pods behind the cockpit.

The master-computer ran Excalibur, which left the pilot little to do, other than monitor instruments and passengers. We settled into the compression couches and the canopies closed over our bodies, to seal us in for the takeoff. The anti-acceleration field wrapped around me like a warm blanket of protection in readiness to increase its protective strength as Excalibur blasted away from the platform.

A few minutes later, the red lights above the cockpit changed to green, which indicated an 'open-hatch' to the vacuum of space and a sudden shudder as the rockets beneath us came to full power.

It lasted a few seconds before total silence fell like a dead-blow and all vibration ceased—we escaped the transition and hurtled toward the distant ball, called Earth.

Protective fields in the pods increased their strength in proportion to the force of the acceleration as the spacecraft strove for the optimum speed of 3000 kilometers per second, about seventy-five percent of its capability.

Once at optimum speed the pod canopies sprung open, the protective effect canceled and left us free to get up and float about in zero-g. Two computerized flight spas, below deck, provided the crew and passengers muscle-tone for their bodies. I felt the need to avoid Uncle Sid and Freda for a while, so I made a beeline for one of the spas with the hope of much needed time to think about my future.

After my workout, I floated back to the passenger area. With everyone else turned in I climbed back into my pod for some shuteye. No real conclusions with regard to my future graced my thoughts, although a my mindset remained—one of fierce resolution—not to take my dad's final words to heart. The message he left would serve one purpose—to make me feel as guilty as hell. Uncle Sid opposed my decision to turn from the responsibility of my father's request but he of all people, should know how I felt about my father, yet out of respect I tried to consider the advice offered.

After nine hours of slumber, I raised my head to peer through the closed transparent canopy. Motionless in the pod adjacent to mine, Freda appeared to be asleep.

I'd grab breakfast from the meal replicator in the small travel lounge area and try to figure out what to do for the rest of my day. A touch on the keypad sprung the cover and my body floated out, over and above Freda's pod.

I hovered for a moment and looked at her face. The sensual curves of the parted lips, displayed a hint of a smile—she looked lovely; the peroxide-streaked black hair and slight flush on the cheeks, combined to provoke a primal urge deep within me.

It lasted for a second but the image of her face lingered in my mind—much longer than needed.

I caught a glimpse of Uncle Sid at a table in the lounge area, opposite the meal replication section. The zero-g bar clamped over his lap kept him in place, which for all short distance space travel, took some adjustment to the way things are usually done. Zero-gravity is weird—it plays havoc with one's sense of balance—of what's up and down. Unlike the Andromeda, which boasts a fifty-five percent Earth gravitational force on the body, zero G makes one feel out of control.

With my usual choice of 'quasar oats' in hand, I floated toward the table where my uncle sat, a special zero-g mug of cafteen in hand.

He glanced up and smiled. "Feeling a bit better about the journey, Beckett?"

"A little, I guess—it's all been so sudden. I'm still trying to catch my breath."

"It's a great shock for both of us, but it is what it is. I have lost a brother who was very dear to me and you have lost a father you feel has in many ways, let you down."

I remained silent and sucked on the straw of my porridge container. Uncle Sid looked up from his mug and fixed me with a sympathetic gaze.

"It may interest you to know, whenever he and I spoke, fifty percent of our conversation was about you."

I peered over my straw. "Instigated by you."

"No—never by me—always by him. He cared very deeply about you and although he experienced disappointments with you not wanting to follow in his footsteps, he came to terms with it—being on the cusp of improving the quality of life for humankind became his driving passion."

"Passionate enough for him to forget he had a son."

43

The president commander leaned back in his seat and continued to eye me while he took a long draft of his drink.

"I doubt you or I will ever understand his motivations but I know in my heart of hearts he loved you. The death of your mother was a terrible blow to him and he never forgave himself."

I remained quiet and continued to suck on the straw with restrained anger—I wanted to say hurtful things but thought better of it.

"Your mother was a lovely, but lonely woman who suffered from depression, and your dad's work was very consuming during those days. He felt he should have been there for her, but the demands from the WGF were so great on him."

The World Genetic Foundation, the outfit my dad worked for and an equal cause of my ruined life, triggered negative thoughts for me. Uncle Sid might as well have waved a red rag before the eyes of a bull, yet I managed to restrain myself.

Deep inside, I hoped he might throw new light on my mother's death. My dad's culpability, spawned by his gross absenteeism, was old news. Uncle Sid tried to cheer her up and I remembered how my mother would mope around when my dad never came home for days on end. It emphasized the reality of their failed relationship.

Sometimes a deeper, more sinister reason haunted my thoughts, fostered by the way my mother and Uncle Sid looked at each other whenever I brought up questions about my father's absence. There remained something between the three of them I knew nothing about.

My uncle continued. "You can't blame it all on the WGF. The Administration also played a part in pushing the WGF for results. The declining populations were causing great concern amongst world leaders and a breakthrough in longevity science promised the continuance of our species."

The Administration also ranked high on my list of hate crime perpetrators. It was the central control agency for the New World Earth executive, a group of selected leaders from around the globe, commissioned with the welfare of the world economy and general life affairs of all nations.

Robotics played a huge role in our management system—fifty percent of the administrators comprised of human beings and fifty percent, android. The growth of artificial Intelligence, in complexity and sophistication, thus granted androids major roles within the affairs of state and general lives of humans, to the point they maintained a balanced presence.

Many people saw this as a threat to humankind. They feared machines would one day wipe us out.

I hated both The Administration and the WGF, and saw them as major contributors to my mother's depression and her suicide.

My father's work brought some hope for the declined birthrate of humans since the Great War of 2135. His brilliant, genetic deductions from the huge amount of time spent on research and experimentation, helped the human race in its recovery to a minus five percent growth rate. The ravages of the war and sterilization from the sun's solar radiation also exacerbated the growth of Earth's population.

But for my dad's efforts, humans would become an extinct species by the year 2500 C.E. I felt conflicted and confused when in contemplation of these issues because it evoked a sense of pride on his behalf—but for me, it always led back to parental absenteeism.

Uncle Sid made to leave. "I need to talk to the pilot. Please check on Freda for me—she hates space flight."

I released my seat's zero-G restraint. "Why do you think she came along?"

"She knew your father for a short period before our maiden voyage to the asteroid belt. She actually worked at the WGF as an Industrial psychologist before I conned her into working for me."

This was news to me, but then, I knew little of the people my dad worked with.

"What's happened to his android?"

"Happydoo? He's still around, as always."

My dad's android, passed down to him by my grandfather, had been in the family for at least 150 years. It was common talk for us to refer to Happydoo as a 'he,' despite his technological origin. My grandfather named him for a unique feature, common to his program—a response to any request always included the phrase; 'I'm happy to do this for you.' The name has stuck for time and eternity—everyone knows him as Happydoo, even Central's android service warehouse reflected this name on all service documentations.

"You should listen to the message your dad left because he detailed some instructions regarding his assets. It all, of course, comes to you, being his sole survivor. You and I will go through his belongings and decide what to do—I hope I can count on you for at least that much."

The words stung but Uncle Sid, not a vindictive person, meant well. His need to have me go through my dad's possessions with him appeared genuine. He pushed off in the direction of the gangway, to disappear in the direction of the flight-deck.

I floated to a viewport and observed the stars. The vastness of space contained an infinite amount of objects, all in silent observation of Excalibur's transit, through the deep blackness—I floated adjacent to the port and held onto a hull-protrusion, transfixed by the sheer beauty and magnificence of the spectacle. Two million kilometers on the port side, the red planet could be seen—a sight to behold.

The window's 'mag-patch,' a special magnification component within its confines, included a zoom feature and I could see the dark specs of several human colonies on the surface of Mars. The Administration, in conjunction with the military initiated the Mar's terraform program about one hundred years ago, but it would take another six hundred years before any sort of breathable atmosphere might support life.

My mind, in complete awe at the pace of the human species propagation and technological sophistication since the Great War, took in the scene. The final frontier lay all around us in deep space. The achievements initiated by the first industrial revolution in the eighteenth century, paled in terms of the latest acquired knowledge.

My intense and silent contemplation came to an abrupt end when a hand grasped my shoulder.

∞∞

Six

More News for the Confused.

Freda hung in the air and with one hand extended, held onto an inner hull support.

"Hi, Freda." My response was hesitant.

"Busy ogling the elegant universe?" she asked.

"Yes—you can see Mars quite clearly."

I moved aside and allowed her access to the magnification patch. She leaned forward, closer to the mag-patch's four-inch square parameter. After a brief look, her fingertips touched the control adjustors on the window to sharpen the image. Again, I could smell a light waft of perfume, and it mesmerized me.

"What a beautiful sight," she exclaimed. "Seeing another planet so close is worth all the trouble of taking the journey."

"I believe you don't enjoy spaceflight that much." I stated the fact more than asked the question.

"No, actually, I have never enjoyed the take-offs and landings but I am used to being in space, obviously. I hardly consider the Andromeda to be 'flying in a spacecraft'—it's so big."

She smiled, the contrast of bright-red lipstick with fair skin, made her face light up like a festive commercial.

"Let's get some cafteen from the replicator. I have something important to tell you."

We each grabbed a zero-g mug and solicited the cafteen, my second—Freda chose porridge for breakfast. We floated back to the table and deployed the zero-G restraints.

She sipped at her cafteen and held my stare for a few moments.

"I'm sure Sid told you I once worked with your dad. Not exactly with him, but for the foundation."

I leaned back and nodded.

"I was responsible for the psychological welfare of the workplace, and part of the job was perusing the personal files of all the staff. I know your mother committed suicide when you were a teen—it was in your dad's file."

"Tell me something I don't know."

Freda's jaw muscles tensed and she lowered her eyes.

"I'm sorry, Beckett, I know this is painful for you but there are certain things about your mother's death that puzzled me. I read the police and coroner reports."

I leaned forward. "What about the reports?"

She hesitated for a brief moment and chose careful words.

"She had become involved with someone else before her death. The reports contained no information on the third person's identity. I have no wish to add to your dilemma, but it's best you know as much of the detail as possible."

∞∞

Seven

Earth
1300 hours, 26th June, 2315 C.E.

The onboard master computer handled the final approach and docked the Excalibur with mathematical precision. To be back on Earth released a torrent of old memories and the earlier talk with Freda, kindled a new stress for me. My mother and I enjoyed a close relationship to the end of her life; despite whatever antipathy I felt for my father, it might be unfair of me to judge him on the mere fault of his career focus.

A sinister thought lurked at the back of my mind and it behooved me to consider the point with some care. If my mother became involved with someone, could that party carry some responsibility for her eventual suicide? I wondered why Uncle Sid never spoke of the matter.

A green light flashed above the flight deck's door and the canopies to our travel-pods flew open and canceled the effects of the anti-acceleration field. The captain waited for us at the exit lock. He shook our hands and spoke a few words with both Uncle Sid and Freda before we passed through the airlock proper. The familiar hiss of pressurized air filled our ears as the outside hatch opened to allow the familiar smells and sounds of the Quantum City spaceport to invade our senses.

We made a beeline for the BCD, or Body Conditioning Spa, where the three of us would spend two hours of 'adjusting' therapy, a mandatory procedure for any returned traveler, who lived in outer-space. It helped reintroduce the human body to the full constraints of the home planet.

We completed our therapy by 1230 hours. Freda's arrangements included our stay at the Orion hotel while we attended to the business of my father's burial. Our bodies also needed time to regain their normal strength.

She finalized the arrangements for my dad's memorial service and planned a short stay at the Eagle's Nest, our family's hideaway, in the Eagle mountain range—property inherited from my grandfather.

Many annual vacations included stopovers at the 'Nest' until my mother died. I returned a few times after that but without the family, there seemed little point.

The Orion impressed me. High-end hotels offered luxurious accommodation which could not be found aboard the Andromeda or on Mars. I settled on the oval bed in my room for a quick rest, my thoughts centered around Freda's unanticipated news, when the light above the door blinked several times—someone appeared to be in the hallway at the entrance to my room. I activated the force-field retraction from the console, situated on the bed's headboard and to my astonishment a man marched in, to stand at the foot of my bed.

'Good afternoon, Master Beckett.'

I failed to recognize the person who stood before me, arms folded and a broad grin, spread across familiar features. The digital purr of the voice, however, brought instant identification and I reacted with spontaneous delight.

"Happydoo—it's been a long time. You look amazing."

The android, my late father's personal valet and member of the Conroy family for longer than I could remember, did a neat pirouette and stomped its one foot on the floor, an action it always performed for the family when complimented.

I noticed changes to Happydoo's aesthetic appearance. He sported synthetic hair in place of the dark-colored cranial plate, of earlier models and there seemed a distinct human-like air of confidence about his attitude; no doubt a providence of the latest upgrade. He wore a normal town suit coverall, spun by a nano-fabricator and could almost be mistaken for a human being.

My mind ranged back to when, as a family, we enjoyed many good times together.

"What nonsense have you been up to, Happydoo?"

My father's favorite question whenever the android returned from

an errand or a chore, always triggered the its routine of self-deprecation and joy.

He responded in the same manner every time. He would raise his bionic knuckles to the synthetic mouth and give an embarrassed chuckle.

Happydoo gave me a quick resume of his most recent escapades and ended with a very mournful look.

'The day I learned of Master Padraig's death had to be the saddest day of my entire existence.'

A machine, who could talk on an emotional level and in a sentient way, warranted my earnest attention. I detected a trace of heartfelt sorrow—damn, those clever AI engineering bastards, deserved my admiration.

"Where were you on the day of his death?"

'I had been taking in an upgrade at central's warehouse, Master Beckett. Master Padraig had decided to send me on the fateful day of his demise. He seemed very tense at the time.'

"Do you think my father was murdered?"

'I have no opinion on the subject at this time, Master Beckett. There is no relevant information for me to make an adequate judgment. I do know he had been harassed by unknown parties before his death.'

Heaven preserve me! I asked a straight forward question and the machine pontificated on the answer.

We talked about old times for another half-hour before I felt

my thoughts gravitate toward rest again. The transition of gravities required an appropriate amount of adjustment time—I could feel my body and mental faculties in an acute decline.

"I feel the need for a quick nap, Happydoo—legacy of a long trip from the asteroid belt—why don't you rejuvenate your processor with a good charge and we can chat later?"

My question solicited the typical response. *'I will be happy to do that, Master Beckett.'*

The android moved to the charge booth, situated adjacent to the ablution chamber. Charge booths accommodated patrons who traveled with their AI valets—a free power service.

I closed my eyes and fell into a deep sleep. Later, the comm-buzzer above my head caused an immediate and unwelcomed interruption. A green comm light winked on the headboard's console.

For a moment I thought to cancel it but intuition induced a change of mind.

"Yes, what is it?"

"Is this Beckett Conroy?"

"Yes, this is Beckett—who am I talking to?"

"I have information regarding your father's death that will interest you—meet me at the cafteen house, directly across from your hotel's entrance, in ten minutes—and come alone."

"Who is this?"

"I will explain everything when we meet—I repeat, come alone. Find a seat, grab a mug of cafteen and wait—I'll come to you."

The comm went silent. I stared at the ceiling and wondered about hallucinations. I jumped off the bed and rushed to the window to view the street, seven stories below. Across the street a sign on the wall read, 'Nick's Cafteen House.'

Should I place a call to Freda, or Uncle Sid, to let them know about the mysterious caller? We all suffered fatigue, however, so I decided against the disturbance of their much needed rest. With Happydoo still connected into the hotel valet charge system it seemed unnecessary to solicit his company. I dressed and left the room.

∞∞

Eight

A Prominent Member of Society

The late afternoon sun shone through the protective, transparent dome overhead and I felt the cooler air, envelope my body. Soon the heat pumps would activate to keep the temperature at a constant twenty degrees Celsius through the night.

Due to a weaker geomagnetic field the construction of graphene glass domes over populated areas became necessary by the early 2300's. The street, reserved for antigravity, emergency vehicles which belonged to either the hospital or The Administration, appeared to be empty. General human traffic, together with androids and bots used the pedestrian escalators and underground magnotrains which ran around the clock, mostly in the direction of suburbs and spaceports. I crossed the street to the place of meeting.

Nick's Cafteen House catered for pre-work, lunchtime and post-working people in need of a hot beverage, or snack. The holographic menu listed several different flavors of cafteen. I ordered a mug of Roseberry and sat to wait.

A few minutes, later two men entered the shop and came straight to my table. One of the men dressed in a fancy pin stripe, nano-suit sat at the table opposite me.

"Good afternoon, Mr. Conroy."

He spoke with a smooth, polite voice. "Thank you for coming. I represent a prominent member of Quantum City society. He has asked me to explain his position to you."

I waited to hear what this 'prominent member of our society' wanted of me. Mr. Pin-stripe's partner looked like a professional of pub-fighter. His mean, tough look and scarred face made me doubt his ability to speak.

Pin-stripe continued. "Your father and the person I represent both had a vested interest in the bio-molecular breakthrough of the century. You are, of course, familiar with the A-Mortal life-extension research your father spearheaded?"

I raised my eyebrows but remained silent.

"A message your father left you, before his untimely death, has come to our attention, and we understand it contains a clue only you would be able to decipher."

My eyes opened in astonishment. "How did the person you represent know about my father's message?"

My outburst did not faze Pin-stripe. "My boss is a well-connected person. It doesn't matter how he found out—he knows."

His words carried an ominous ring and warning bells clanged in my ears.

"With his vested interest in the research, he has asked me to propose a deal whereby you both will benefit from the proceeds of the discovery if it proves scientifically viable."

My hackles rose. "He wants to make a deal with me—to muscle in on my father's discovery?"

Pin-stripe looked a little peeved. "It's not called 'muscling in,' Mr. Conroy—it's called 'making a deal' on behalf of an interest with which he has been involved for many years."

"He works for the WGF?" I asked.

"I am not at liberty to say, however, you can bank on one thing—if you don't accept his generous offer, there will be certain repercussions."

Up to this point my responses contained an element of politeness, however, Pin-stripe's threat got to me and my anger surfaced.

"Understand this, shithead. I'll not be threatened, or bought off. You can tell your boss to forget any deal. My father made it clear I would be the one who would follow up on the research."

My outburst surprised me. The decision of involvement in my dad's work still remained a matter for consideration but no one outside my family circle would be a free-loader and benefit from his hard work. The intent of this pompous, prominent member of society became clear—the veiled threat in Pin-stripe's message told its own tale. I stood and made to leave.

"This little charade is over."

Pin-stripe's ugly, muscled goon stood in my path. His broad shoulders and barrel chest sent a formidable message. Pin-stripe motioned him to step aside and let me leave.

"Don't say I didn't warn you, Mr. Conroy."

"I don't deal with shitheads," I said.

"You haven't even heard what my boss has proposed," he complained.

"Tell your boss to stick his proposal up his ass."

I left Nick's and crossed the street to the Orion.

*

In the hotel's foyer, an anxious Freda met me.

"Beckett, we've been so worried about you—did you go out for a walk?"

"You could say that. Do you know where my uncle is?"

"He stepped out—said he had some things to attend to."

The slow abatement of anger helped to settle my thoughts and I made a conscious decision to dismiss the discussion with Pin-stripe for the time being.

"My father's valet, Happydoo arrived this morning. He's in my room getting charged up."

"How wonderful. I remember the android from one of my visits with Sid. He is so amusing."

"Yeah, well, I guess I'll inherit him. There's no one else in the family but Uncle Sid and myself."

Freda shot me a wistful glance. "I feel like a drink—would you like to join me in the bar after I've freshened up a little? Let's make it in half an hour."

It seemed a good idea to me. "I'd love to—I'll be down in thirty minutes."

Back in my room, Happydoo greeted me with enthusiasm. I decided to ask the android to play back my father's message from its active memory drive. After my nano-suit unraveled I kicked off my shoes and lay on the bed.

"So what's this message my father left for me?"

The android smiled. *'I can relay the message straight from his CCT if you like, Master Beckett.'*

"Thanks, the personal touch is always better."

A cerebral cortex transmitter or CCT, allowed a human to communicate with robotic equipment. The transmission of specific thought-signals from the brain, to a receiver located in a robot's processor, could be facilitated by a thought command system. The transmitter clipped onto the outer ear and made contact with the human temple, via a small pad. A robotic receiver picked up the signals and converted them into real words within the robot's processor. Real words could then be recited verbatim and in the originator's voice by the robot, to a third party.

Happydoo performed his pirouette and foot-stomp routine for my benefit. It always delighted me as a young boy, to witness the act and now as an adult, I appreciated it even more. I felt a sudden affection for the android—it would now become my personal valet.

I waited for Happydoo to deliver the anticipated dispatch and when it came, nothing could have prepared me for the experience.

∞∞

Nine

Padraig Conroy Speaks

The sound of my dad's voice took me by surprise; I expected Happydoo to repeat the message in his own digital purr but instead Padraig Conroy spoke from the grave. A Conflict of emotions erupted within my soul. The long-awaited message turned out to be more than I bargained for:

Beckett, I may not be around when you finally get to hear this. I know things have been strained between us for many years, but I want you to know I have always loved you dearly. I take the blame for the break in our relationship. Your mother and I were so blessed to have you as part of our family. Please forgive me for the neglect of my parental duty toward you, but I think you and I are very like-minded. We are both strong-willed with reclusive tendencies. We also have excellent minds which can focus, and when they do, it's to the detriment of everything else.

I am on the cusp of a breakthrough that will revolutionize human life forever. I am so close to the most incredible discovery in human history, but there is a problem—someone else knows—someone who wants to use it for selfish commercial gain. I have taken my research underground, because I don't know who I can trust at the foundation.

Right at this very moment, I am being stalked. Happydoo will find you and relay the situation as it is so far. The research is in a place only you will be able to find. I have erased the research's hiding place from Happydoo's memory bank so no one can use him to discover its location. You will have to work it out.

Whatever grudge you carry because of my selfishness is fully warranted—I'm a lousy father. I understand you will probably want nothing to do with my work, but this breakthrough is much bigger than our mutual problem. I believe you have the intelligence, training, and fortitude to continue the work I have started. It will make you famous but I must warn you—those stalking me will also stalk you. Be vigilant and trust only people you know. Your uncle Sid and I have had our differences but he has always been the father to you that I should have been, and for that I applaud him—but be aware, he too has his ambitions.

You are probably wondering how you will find my research material—I'm sorry I have to be so clandestine. I know it make's things difficult, but what is difficult for you will be almost impossible for the enemy. Watch your back. There are those who will kill to get their hands on my research.

You should be able to work out the location from the following verse—but remember—not all is as it seems.

In a time long ago, he died from a fall
While looking for eggs in the nest.
The info-vial is important but in the end
Your valet will pass the test.

I love you, son.

His voice choked at the end and tears welled up in my eyes. I reached for nose-wipes on a shelf, adjacent to the bed. After my composure settled, I made ready to meet with Freda. The wall chrono revealed it had been almost an hour since I last spoke to her.

∞∞

Ten

Freda

2145 hours, 26th June, 2315 C.E.

Freda sat at the bar counter with glass of whiskey in hand.

"Did you get distracted?"

"I'm sorry—time on the odd occasion seems to get away from me," I said.

"That's very understandable under the present circumstances. You must have a lot on your mind."

My father's voice still haunted me. His final words, not to trust anyone unless I knew them well, made me suspicious of everybody. It dawned on me—I didn't know anyone 'really well' anymore. The result of four months in space placed a limit on any communications with my few friends on Earth. I couldn't think of one relationship on the home planet with which contact still prevailed.

Again, my father's voice: '*You and I are very like-minded...*'

"Where are you, right now?" Freda asked.

The question came as no surprise. Not that I didn't want to chat over a casual drink, but could I trust her with the contents of my father's communication?

My eyes must have glazed over for a moment. A gut-feel, the trusty ally of my intuition, suggested Freda would always be my friend. She revealed more to me about the status quo than Uncle Sid ever did.

The android bartender appeared so I ordered my drink. Freda leaned closer and stared into my eyes.

"Are you okay, Beckett? You seem to be a little pale around the gills."

After a brief hesitation I made a decision to trust her.

"I had a frank conversation this afternoon with someone who appears to have an unhealthy interested in my father's business."

Freda raised her brows and set her drink on the counter.

I continued. "There were two of them—they said their boss had a vested interest in the breakthrough and wanted to make me a deal for the information on the discovery."

"Where did you meet with them?"

"Across the road in Nick's Cafteen House."

I shared the story of my confrontation and ended with the contents of Dad's message, but left out the clue—a dynamic, which still awaited my contemplation. This required a walk down memory's lane, to a time when my dad and I enjoyed a close relationship—a small and much-loved boy, with whom he played many a word game.

It is my belief Dad knew the identity of his adversaries. These dangerous people would stop at nothing to achieve their goals.   It dawned on me—my life would be in great danger if the mystery of the clue became resolved.

Pin-stripe and his ugly partner did not allow me to go free out of the kindness of their black hearts. I happen to be their most valuable asset. This state of affairs, however, would end once the details of the discovery passed into their hands. I would be expendable.

Freda's face conveyed a picture of conflicted emotions. She placed her hand over mine.

"I want you to know you can trust me, Beckett. I knew something was up when Sid first broke the news of your dad's death."

A fear suddenly gripped me.

"I'm not sure what to do—if I decide to follow up on this clue it will place my life in danger—our lives, you and Uncle Sid, as well."

She moved closer and I could almost taste the musky fragrance of her skin. The beautiful eyes searched for a more intimate connection and her sensual lips, so close to mine, begged contact. It was not to be.

"There you two are! I knocked on both your doors to no avail—I thought you might be down here."

Sid Conroy pushed passed the other people seated at the bar counter to

take up an empty seat beside Freda. He motioned to the bartender, asked for a glass of cold water and leaned forward to look at me.

"So, what happened to you this afternoon, Beckett?"

Encouraged by my conversation with Freda, I related my episode with the two shitheads, after which he took a quiet moment to sip on the glass of water and assess the situation.

"Are you okay—did the swine hurt you?"

"Fortunately, no. I'm good. There is an implied threat, though."

My uncle shifted in his seat. "I was worried your father's assailants would try to glean information from you. It's an obvious consideration—your dad would try to get you involved, seeing you are to a degree, qualified in bio-molecular genetics."

Freda jumped into the conversation. "Who are these people? Do you think Padraig knew them?"

Uncle Sid weighed the question. "I'm not sure. He never spoke to me of anyone who might be a threat. I didn't know he was working on something

so important."

"Maybe it's someone he worked with—someone who might have access to his research," Freda replied. A deep frown creased the silky-white skin of her forehead.

"The shithead, who confronted me today, implied his boss had a 'vested interest' in the discovery. When I asked if his boss worked for the WGF, he wouldn't say."

Uncle Sid leaned back in his chair. "It certainly sounds as though it would be one of your father's colleagues."

Part of the course on genetics, received by memory induction at the Learning Institute, touched on the history of patents and licenses required for important discoveries.

"I do know a little about the procedures the foundation would follow, regarding research of this nature. It would have been classified top secret and only a very limited group would have access to the information."

Freda scowled. "The question is what action do we take? Should we go to the authorities?"

Uncle Sid cocked his head to one side, "and tell them what?—some unknown entity is after Padraig Conroy's research? We have no proof of anything."

Freda looked a little deflated. "There must be something we can do. I'm worried they may try again and this time Beckett might not be so fortunate."

This reminded Uncle Sid of the clue. "Have you thought about the clue, Beckett—does it make any sense?"

"Not really—I have to think about it—it doesn't ring any bells at the moment."

"Are you not going to do anything about finding your father's murderers?" asked Freda. Her tone contained a measure of indignation.

No apparent action came to my mind. "We have to remind ourselves of one thing—we are still not one hundred percent sure about the cause of his death. I will give it some thought, but right now, I'm going to get a good night's sleep—if that's even possible."

Uncle Sid turned to Freda. "Have you been able to make arrangements for the memorial?"

"I have booked the chapel at the city's main cremation facility for the 29th. A notice has also been placed on the Omninet for 1500 hours on the same day. The service will be presided over by a Mr. Burk—the chief remains disposal supervisor. I also spoke to a Miss Carla Jensen at the foundation—she said to get there about 1400 hours to-morrow and you can meet with the chairman of the board."

"Well, that's the main reason why we are here. Thank you, Freda. Was there anything else we needed to do?"

Freda recalled one more arrangement she had made.

"I called the city mortuary and they said we could view Padraig's body any time in the late af-ternoon tomorrow."

This came as a bit of a shock. In the recess of my mind I knew it needed to be done. Visions of my mother's body still haunted me and now I would have to contend with his corpse as well.

Uncle Sid read my thoughts. "Bear up, Beckett—it's something we have to do."

The palms of my hands broke into a sweat as I nodded and swallowed the last of my drink. We all stood to take our leave.

Uncle Sid took my elbow as the three of us walked together toward the nearest verticap.

"Tomorrow morning the three of us should go to your father's apartment and decide what to do with his things. We also need to drop in at the foundation—he probably had a personal locker—who knows what we may discover."

I agreed and terminated any further discussion about the matter. Freda grabbed my hand and gave it a squeeze as we exited the verticap.

"Try to get some sleep. Beckett. Your mind will try to lead you down the rabbit hole if you allow it."

I knew what she meant. "See you in the morning."

My eyes followed her as she walked away. The hour-glass shape of her figure, accentuated by the tight nano-fabric suit, made me want to be with her—to share her bed and perform sensual acts of love. It took an effort to subdue the mental images in my mind and deny my obvious need.

Uncle Sid must have clued into my thoughts.

"She's quite refreshing isn't she?"

"Yes, she is—you are lucky to have her as your assistant."

"You don't want to be near her when she catches a downswing, though."

"I consider myself forewarned."

Back in my room, the consideration vanished and I thought about our intimacy at the bar counter—how close I came to the kiss, which would have opened the Pandora's box of my mind.

∞∞

Eleven

My Father's Apartment

In the morning everyone appeared hale and hearty in the Orion's dining facility, ready for breakfast. After our meal we spoke about the events of the previous day and at 10:00 hours, left the hotel.

We took the sidewalk escalator in the direction of Quantum Ridge, the area where all level-one appointees lived.

The system of appointed status in the New World Earth system vexed me to a point. I, as a level-four, could not live in a level-one appointed district, unless I stayed with someone of that status. The appointments, tokens of seniority and position within the main industries of the world system, came under regular scrutiny by Central, the master quantum computer. The Administration regulated the appointments of everyone's living space and conferred special treatment to those who contributed to the work effort.

Finally my dad's apartment block came into view and we clambered into the verticap for transport to floor one hundred ten—unit 1105. I had not been here in at least ten years. The times I saw my father, after the completion of my education at the NWE Learning Institute, could be counted on one hand.

The morning flew by while Uncle Sid and I, under Freda's supervision, went through all my dad's belongings. Happydoo contented himself to lift and carry while I opened cartons to pull out items for Freda to look at. By 1300 hours, three piles remained on the floor—personal items, recycling and garbage.

My dad did not collect a great deal of material sentimentalities due to work focus, which left no time for extravagances. Happydoo assured us there was nothing of any real value, and what could not be recycled or thrown away, should be left for the future occupant—I felt comfortable with this approach.

Freda looked around her. "It's such a shame—he was such a good man—he was such a major contributor."

Surprised by her comment I reacted with a negative tone.

"Contributor?"

She rounded on me with flushed face. "Yes, Beckett—contributor! Your father has done wonders in the field of molecular biology and genetics—saved countless lives and given us all the chance to live much longer."

I took a step back and decided discretion would be the better path forward in the conversation.

"You are absolutely right, of course."

She glanced at the floor and for a moment it appeared she might burst into tears. My guilt produced pangs of remorse for the poor attitude I displayed toward my father and to show empathy, placed my arm around her shoulders. She turned toward me and buried her face in my chest. Uncle Sid raised his eyebrows and moved off to the balcony. Happydoo cocked his head to one side.

'Is everything in order, Master Beckett?'

My dry throat managed a few croaky words.

"Everything's fine, Happydoo—let's finish up."

'I am happy to do that, Master Beckett.'

Freda lifted her chin and our eyes met. The converging of lips came more by reflex than intentional action. Her bright-red lipstick tasted sweet as she clasped the back of my head with one hand and craned her neck to apply a hungry pressure as our tongues entwined. Shocked at the urgency conveyed by the gesture, I knew it did not bode well for my bachelor approach to life.

The kiss lingered before she withdrew and buried her face into my chest again. We stood like two statues in an embrace until Happydoo completed his assigned task. The android cocked its head again, in quizzical inquiry. *'Are we ready to leave, Master Beckett?'*

I let go of Freda. Uncle Sid returned from the balcony to witness my vain attempts to remove Freda's lipstick from my lips and raised his eyebrows.

I hunched my shoulders as a sign of my own confusion and turned to the front entrance.

"Let's get out of here. We still need to pay a visit to the Foundation."

∞∞

Twelve

The World Genetic Foundation

Freda needed to return to the hotel so I asked Happydoo to accompany her. In a way, a sense of relief permeated my thoughts regarding Freda's presence. The impromptu kiss left me a little confused—I needed time to think about our future relationship. The idea of commitment still bothered me.

We arrived at the WGF reception and Uncle Sid introduced me as Padraig Conroy's son. He asked to see the chairman of the board. No names of any of my dad's associates came to my mind, and I realized how little I knew of his affairs.

The receptionist called upstairs and received a swift answer to our enquiry.

"Dr. Jameson will see you straight away. Take the verticap to the twentieth floor and his secretary will be there, waiting."

We stepped out onto the twentieth floor furnished with a plush wall-to-wall carpet and beautiful holographic pictures of pristine country-side, which no longer existed on Earth.

A woman waited to lead the way to the director's office. I judged her to be in her late twenties and dressed in a smart red, nano-fibre suit she presented a stunning picture of beauty.

"My name is Carla. Please follow me, Dr. Jameson is waiting."

I could not help but gawp at the slim figure and the elegant poise with which she carried herself. Long blond hair hung down to the trim waist and her well-defined ass swung in rhythmical fashion, from side to side. My eyes became mesmerized and when she stopped at a large opaque force-field entrance, I almost crashed into the back of her. She stepped aside and gave me a cheeky smile. My heart did a double flip and I could only gaze at her with a foolish lob-sided grin.

Carla tapped the key of a wall-mounted pad as we waited. A tiny camera swiveled toward our position and a voice sounded from above our heads. "Bring them in, Carla."

The force field retracted to reveal a huge office area with a large desk at the far end. Three people stood as we approached—the man in the center came around the end of the desk to greet us with hand extended.

He clasped Uncle Sid's outstretched hand. "I am so sorry for your loss, Mr. Conroy—and this must be young Beckett."

Stooped with age and gaunt in face, Jameson's voice sounded frail. His eyes smoldered like two dark coals in sunken sockets, and I guessed his age to be about one hundred thirty-five years.

"These are my two colleagues, Dr. Sutton and Dr. Nassir. Dr. Sutton is in charge of the Department of Molecular Biology under which the Department of Genetics is a division—he worked very closely with your father."

Dr. Sutton, an obese man with flabby jowls shook hands, first with Uncle Sid and then me. The third man waited for his turn.

"Dr. Nassir, head of Consciousness Engineering and Neurobiology."

Dr. Nassir's dark, sallow skin sketched his ancient Arabic background. A long pointed nose and thick bushy eyebrows accentuated his features.

"I worked very closely with Dr. Conroy—we all did. I can't tell you how much we are going to miss him—his leadership impressed everyone in the WGF."

Dr. Nassir's words caused a bell to ring in my brain. Could this be the 'prominent member of society' who boasted a vested interest in my dad's affairs? Dr. Jameson moved back to his seat behind the desk and motioned us all to take a seat. The atmosphere of formality gave the impression the three academics wanted us out of their hair as soon as possible.

The old man leaned back in his seat and looked at the two of us.

"I am glad you've popped in to see us today. We've been discussing the best route to finalizing Dr. Conroy's research, which Dr. Nassir believes was on the verge of a monumental discovery."

Sutton leaned forward, his brow furrowed like a ploughed section of soil. "The problem is the final details of his research are missing. We understand that paranoia regarding his work being stolen for commercial exploitation might have been uppermost in Padraig's mind."

Uncle Sid, with elbows braced on the arm-rests of the chair, placed both hands together to form a steeple with his fingers.

"How so?"

Nassir stepped in, his eyes narrowed and thoughtful.

"We have reason to believe some unknown person had made a threat—this caused your brother to remove his final research and continue it underground."

The conversation drifted toward some sort of accusation with regard to my dad's culpability for the loss of the discovery by reason of paranoia. My ire rose. These over-stuffed, academic dummies knew shit about my dad. They sat in pontification over the loss of a discovery, instead of my dad's demise. I could feel a shift in my attitude toward my father—my kin, my flesh and blood. These sanctimonious bastards discussed his life with such glibness—it made my skin crawl, but I held my cool.

Jameson must have detected my annoyance and cut in.

"There may well have been a threat made, and I can understand his protectiveness of the work. It would be a great help to all of humankind if we could find that missing research and complete the discovery."

Sutton scratched at a jowl and glanced at me.

"Your father didn't perhaps contact you, or leave any message regarding his final research?"

"My father and I rarely spoke to each other—I have heard nothing from him," I lied.

Uncle Sid backed me up. "We haven't heard from Padraig for some time. He suffered a reclusive nature—ever since the death of his wife."

Nassir's voice carried a patronizing tone.

"Ah, yes—the death of his wife!"

I wanted to jump up and strangle him, but Uncle Sid placed his hand on my arm to restrain me.

"Well, if you find anything during your stay, or before you go back into space. What is it you do?—galactic mining? Please don't hesitate to contact us."

The little we could offer made us dispensable. I felt like I needed a demisting, a complete refurbish of my stomach lining. Jameson stood with slow deliberation and held onto the desk. His coal-black eyes focused on me.

"I believe you have been through the bio-molecular genetics and neuro-science program offered by the NWE Institute?"

I nodded.

"If you ever feel you want to continue in your dad's footsteps, please call me—I'm sure the apple doesn't fall far from the tree."

The others did not stand or offer hands to shake in farewell, which suited me fine. I already felt my hand needed to be disinfected. Dr. Jameson touched the keypad on his desktop and the opaque field opened to let us through. Glad to escape the stifled atmosphere of the office we made a bee-line for the exit—should the meeting have continued for any greater length of time I might have needed medical attention, but providence spared us.

Uncle Sid grabbed my arm to hurry me along. It seemed he felt the same way. We rounded a corner in the long hallway and made for the verticap. While we waited for the capsule to arrive, a voice called out my name.

I swiveled on my heels to be greeted by the immaculate persona of Carla Jensen. She ran up to me and thrust a card into my hand, turned and walked away. I stared after her with wide eyes as the verticap buzzer sounded.

We overcame inertia to step into the capsule and I glanced at the card. Her name, with a photograph and an omninet contact number on the one side caught my eye. I turned the card over in my hand to read a hastily scribbled sentence on the back:

I can help you in your search!

∞∞

Thirteen

Viewing My Father's Remains
1450 hours, 27th June, 2315 C.E.

I showed the card to Uncle Sid. He scrutinized it with the eye of a gem merchant and then handed it back.

For a second or two we traveled in silence before he commented.

"You need to contact her as soon as possible."

The verticap reached ground level and we stepped out into the foyer. I knew the most difficult task of the day still lay ahead—the identification of my late father's body. I felt no repugnance with regard to the viewing, but hesitancy clawed at my resolve, perhaps the residue of an overstrained emotional state. The visit should, however, create closure and allow me to get on with my life.

The escalator outside the WGF entrance bustled with people, bots, and androids. We embarked in the direction of the Quantum City mortuary, situated in the city police department building and after ten minutes stepped off the escalator at the Police Department. People of all types thronged the front entrance to the administration section and it looked more like a central magno-train station. Uncle Sid and I pushed through toward the back of the building where a holographic sign, "Mortuary", indicated the entrance. The surroundings evoked horrid memories—after my mother committed suicide my father and I spent almost a whole day in the place. Nothing appeared to have changed from how I remembered it. We waited in a short lineup to talk to an administrator.

The clerk told us to go down the steps to examination Room C, a cold and sterile chamber, filled with tables upon which cadavers rested. I steeled myself for the dreaded purpose of our visit.

I could understand why Freda declined to accompany us to this macabre and depressed shrine. It oozed the aggressiveness of death's final onslaught against the frailty of human existence. A sense of finality in the atmosphere induced a sadness beyond description.

Room C turned out to be a short walk along a hallway with no windows. The halogen illuminated room contained a counter which blocked any farther progress and a woman, with dark hair, tucked into a net sat with a holographic file on the holo-platform, as we approached.

"Can I help you, gentlemen?"

The tediousness of her job showed in the bored, expressionless voice.

Determined to prove my capability and handle the proceedings I took the lead and told her our names.

"Oh, yes—you are looking for Dr. Conroy from the WGF?"

Her eyes lit up as she motioned us to move around the far end of the counter.

"The autopsy was completed yesterday and the body is ready for the mortician. Please come this way."

She led us to a bank of cadaver containers and pulled on a handle. A tray slid out and heralded the arrival of the dreaded moment.

She pulled the sheet aside to reveal the head and face of my father. Even in death he looked handsome. With morbid confusion, I stared down at his face and couldn't get over how peaceful he appeared. The age lines around his eyes appeared smooth and the lips formed a hint of a smile.

Uncle Sid stood by my side with one hand on my shoulder and we said our goodbyes. I could see the pain written on his face. Despite some differences of opinion over the many years of their relationship, they shared one very real, common bond—me.

"Are we able to get access to the coroner's report?" I asked.

"You will have to stop at the Head Coroner's office. I doubt whether it will be available yet but you can try."

I nodded and she looked at us with impersonal eyes; the look which begged the question: 'have you seen enough?'

I looked at Uncle Sid and he nodded. The sheet was pulled back into place and a sudden panic seized me when it became evident I would never see him again. Suddenly all my anger, confusion, and petulance with regard to our troubled relationship, diminished down a hole the size of a needle's eye. I could not contain my emotions any longer and became human—pent up tears of grief flowed down my cheeks. I fled the room and left Uncle Sid and the woman—their concerned stares followed in my wake.

My headlong flight featured one unrestrained purpose—to escape the atmosphere of the morgue.

At the front entrance I slipped outside, onto the open stairs and made my way to the side of the building, out into the open air. My chest heaved for several moments until the emotion subsided and left me breathless.

I leaned against the outside wall of the police department building and waited for Uncle Sid to find me. He appeared after a while—a worried frown creased his brow.

"Are you okay, son?"

"Yeah. Sorry about that, but it all caught up with me when I looked at his face."

"Not to worry, Beckett. Time is the healer—despite your prior feelings about his parental absenteeism you can rest assured he loved you."

Uncle Sid's words sank in. There seemed no reason for me not to believe him. With my dad's death came the redundancy of a struggle which consumed far too much of my life's energy. Tomorrow, the memorial service would bring a final closure on this issue.

There could not, however, be complete closure until someone solved the mysteries that surrounded the deaths of both parents—the million-dollar question—would that someone be me? Armed with evidence of foul play, it was not yet a certainty my life needed to be complicated with the details. Any further discovery on these issues would not bring my parents back.

We embarked on the escalator in the direction of the Orion. After the earlier escapade with Freda, I felt a little self-conscious about looking her in the eye again. It would be better to keep a low profile until we spaced back to the Andromeda. The scheduled return on the fourth of July would allow the three of us to spend a few days at the hideaway in the Eagle Mountains. Shit,—that could be awkward!

∞∞

Fourteen

Alone with Freda

Back at the Orion, Uncle Sid went to his room and left me free to do the same—or go to the bar for a drink. A wash and change of clothes felt desirable, so I went straight to my room. Happydoo greeted me with the usual, predictable greeting.

'I'm happy to see you, Master Beckett. Is there anything I can do for you?'

"Nothing, thank you, Happydoo. What nonsense have you been up to while I was away?"

Happydoo did the classic knuckle-bite and pirouette routine for my amusement—it seemed, in time, I would become quite fond of him.

*

Dinner time arrived and after a cleanup I plucked up the courage to meet with Freda and

Uncle Sid in the dining room. Freda showed no sign of concern over the morning's episode and greeted me with an upbeat tone of voice. We talked about our WGF visit, followed by the viewing of my dad's body and I told her about my traumatic experience.

"Do you feel you have some closure?" she asked.

"I do feel it helped to put things in to perspective. The problem of resolving how he died still remains an issue though, and after that meeting yesterday with those two shitheads, I'm inclined to think there has been foul play."

Uncle Sid agreed. "I didn't like the attitude of the WGF directors—in particular, that Dr. Nassir. I wouldn't put it past him to be involved in all this."

The arrived of our meals, on the miniature conveyor system interrupted the conversation. A miniature conveyor delivered the orders from food replicators in the kitchen to each table in the dining hall. This system of food delivery fascinated me as we did not have anything like it on the Andromeda. We ate in a tangible silence, preoccupied with the details of the conversation. I felt a tang of self-consciousness invade my thoughts when the occasional glance at Freda drew no attention from her.

With dinner over Uncle Sid bade us good-night.

"I have had quite an emotionally draining day and it's bed time for me. I'll see you both in the morning."

He stood to leave and we bade him a good night. I looked across at Freda and asked if she would like to have a nightcap at the bar before we called it a day.

"I would love to, thank you, Beckett."

I suspected she might feel an obligation to clear the air and my guard came down as we moved to the bar counter. The android bartender took our order—whiskey and soda.

Freda leaned forward on her stool. "So the secretary at the WGF has offered to help with in-formation—do you know what she meant by in-formation?"

"I haven't a clue. Perhaps it means the bulk of the research record, or she might know something about the threats my dad received."

The bartender brought the drinks. Freda gripped the stem of the glass and took a quick sip.

"Have you decided what you are going to do?"

I shifted my weight on the stool and observed the glass in my hand.

"Not right at this moment—no, but when the memorial service is over I'll make a definite decision."

"You'll have Sid's complete support—and mine too, should you decide to follow up on our suspicions."

I found it difficult to look her in the eye. "And if I decide to leave it and get on with my life?"

"That will be your decision to make, but I think Sid would be disappointed."

The bar filled up with hotel patrons and others on a night out. In one corner a rowdy element made lurid jokes and obscene gestures to one another and on an impulse I said to Freda, "Let's grab a bottle and finish our conversation upstairs."

She raised an eyebrow and gave me a mischievous smile. I ordered a bottle of Supernova, and we walked out of the bar and along the hallway, to wait for a verticap.

"Your room or mine?" Freda asked.

"Yours—I think we can do without the firm guidance of dear old Happydoo."

She laughed out loud and gave me a playful shove as the verticap arrived. We stepped into the capsule like two giggling school children. The thought of the android as a chaperon gave cause for much mirth and hilarity.

Freda leaned against me as the capsule zipped to the seventh floor. The smell of her perfume invaded my olfactory senses and mingled with the psycho-neural effect of the alcohol. The result made me feel quite light-headed but, nevertheless, a tonic for the soul, in consideration of the day's accumulated emotional strain.

I felt an intimacy with Freda—a kinship and tenderness one feels for someone who has endured a mutual suffering. She looked up at me with large, soulful eyes and for a second we both became lost in the moment. The kiss was long and investigative. It offered a promise of physical and emotional release. The thoughts for the future—of consequences and commitments became insignificant and the tide of passion swept away all cautious resolve.

We stepped out of the verticap at the chosen destination which required a brief return to the real world. With arms draped around each other's bodies and lips glued together we swerved, lunged, and danced along the hallway to Freda's room.

On arrival at the door she jabbed around the entrance with her thumb until, by pure chance, the entrance control pad received sufficient pressure to release the force field. We fell through the entrance with uncontrollable laughter and collapsed in a heap on the bed, still entangled in each other's limbs. I rolled on top of her and we stared into one another's eyes.

Under the gentle persuasion of my nimble fingers I lifted the nano-fabric control situated around the neck. The entire garment began to unravel and for a few seconds my body needed to raise a few millimeters for the fabric to allow it to fall away onto the bed beside us.

The corners of her mouth turned upward as she undid the clasp of my suit and in a short span of time we both lay naked. I stroked her hair with one hand and cupped her breast with the other to caress the nipple with my tongue. Engulfed with pleasure, our bodies moved against each other with our lips in a desperate, passionate collision.

The bottle of Supernova lay unopened on the bed alongside us, completely forgotten. We moved in the rhythmical beat of love's greatest sacrament with the inevitable conclusion of pleasurable groans and satisfaction. We reached the climax of our passion with an extended moment of gratification, which took several moments to subside. Only the sounds of heavy breathing remained.

We lay there totally engrossed in the moment. I rolled onto my back, to allow my cardiac-rhythm to normalize and reflected on the encounter. Freda lay spread-eagled beside me, her eyes fixed on some imaginary spot on the ceiling and a contented smile adorned her moist lips.

A pang of anxiety presented itself in thoughts for the future—the afflicted mind of this lovely creature beside me, might make a future relationship difficult for us.

Her disorder came to mind, but I could not recall any manifested systems since the beginnings of our travels together, however these symptoms must have erupted at various times in the past or Uncle Sid would not have warned me the night before. Another question shot into my mind: Why was she still un-attached?

Freda faced me and held my stare. "Are you regretting it?"

Taken a bit by surprise, the dismay must have shown on my face.

She rose up on her elbows. "We both needed this—maybe for different reasons, but we needed it."

"What do you mean?"

"I haven't seen you with anyone during your stay on the Andromeda. A man needs a woman, from time to time."

Her logic seemed reasonably sound about my need.

"But what about you, doesn't a woman also need a man?"

She blushed and looked at the ceiling. "I'm sure you can tell I have feelings for you, but don't worry, I'm not trying to extract any sort of commitment."

It became evident my muse regarding her attraction to me held water.

"I really like you, Freda, and I would love for us to be more than friends but you're right—I'm not ready for a serious commitment right now."

I reached up my hand to touch her cheek. She appeared to be on the verge of tears and I feared the worst, which would be a slide into bipolar depression, but with a sudden smile she grabbed my fingers.

"That's okay, Beck. Perhaps I'm not ready either—however, it doesn't mean we can't be friends—one day something might come of it."

I nodded in relief and continued to hold her hand.

"I guess I should get back to my room—I'll see you in the morning."

I stepped up to the auto-dress fabricator and keyed in the instruction for a bathrobe. The hour seemed late and there should be few people about in the hallways; I wanted to get back to my room.

Freda placed her arms around my waist. "See you at breakfast."

I hugged her close for several seconds and then picked up my old suit from the floor to drop it in the used nano-fabric recycle bin.

"You bet." I said.

∞∞

Fifteen

The Final Goodbye
1500 hours, 28th June, 2315 C.E.

Mr. Burk, the remains-disposal supervisor for the Quantum City Life and Death Registry, glanced over the small gathering in the chapel. My general impression of the sad mien he displayed bordered on sanctimonious charlatanism.

It pained me to watch his overdone hand-actions and hear his pious speeches. For this charade the man made five times the amount of credits I made in a year through my training job on the Andromeda.

Besides Uncle Sid, Freda, and myself, the three directors of the WGF and Carla Jensen, all took up the first two rows of seats. Three other unknowns, two men and a woman sat behind us, possibly my dad's colleagues—he appeared to have few friends. One other man sat to the left, outside the main group, under the assaulted of Mr. Burk. He didn't seem to have any association with the WGF but the small aluminum carrycase at his side, indicated him to be in the legal profession. He appeared to be a lawyer. I knew the estate would need to have legal representation with the NWE Administration, plus my father's retention of a lawyer after my mother's death. Uncle Sid saw me glance at the man and whispered in my ear.

"Our lawyer."

At the conclusion of the service the three WGF directors shook hands with us and repeated their condolences. The three unknowns also passed by on their way out, to make mention of their names and association with my dad. Carla Jensen, dressed in a sexy, sleek suit, waited for the others to leave. She came straight to me and took my hand and her touch like a feather, caressed my fingers.

"My offer still stands. Whenever you are ready to follow up on your dad's research, I will help."

"What exactly is it you can help me with?" I asked.

Out of the corner of my eye I saw Freda looking at us.

Carla held onto my hand as we spoke. "I have the research file containing everything re-garding the research—excluding the final results—if you intend to follow up on the potential discovery, you'll need it."

"What about the suspicions regarding his death?"

"I could try to help you there, as well."

I wanted to hear more, but Freda made a move toward us.

"I have a few days before we space back to the Andromeda, the galactic mining craft I work on. Can we meet tomorrow—Nick's Cafteen House, across from the Orion, at say, 0900 hours?"

"Yes, I have a few days off—I can be there."

"Thank you, Carla—I look forward to it."

She gave the slightest suggestion of a smile and let go of my hand. The touch of her fingers in mine, combined with a fragile fragrance of lilacs in bloom, caused a strong, sensual arousal within me as she walked away.

Freda, wearing a frown, pounced on me. "Let me guess; Carla Jensen? Gosh, she's a gorgeous chick."

I smiled and said nothing.

"Did you make an arrangement to meet with her?"

"Tomorrow, Nick's Cafteen House, at 0900 hours."

Freda compressed her lips into a thin smile. "You'll have to watch yourself with her."

"Jealous?" I asked.

"Of course not, silly—but I am concerned her beauty will have you eating out of her hand."

"Not likely," I lied.

I felt a rumble in my gut and realized I needed to eat something so we moved to the refreshments table. Freda stood beside me while I stuffed a slice of cake into my mouth.

The lawyer chose the moment to approach us.

"Beckett Conroy? Could I have a quick word with you?"

He looked at Freda. "My apologies for the interruption, Miss Banning—but I need to discuss some private business in regard to the late Dr. Conroy's estate—could you please excuse us?"

Freda frowned but bowed out to allow the lawyer and I some peace.

He introduced himself as Tom Callas, senior member of a small law firm in Quantum City.

"Your father retained me to take care of his financial concerns, estate, and intellectual property. I have known him for a long time—in fact, I remember you as a young boy, before the unfortunate death of your mother."

Callas seemed to be a genuine person with a longtime interest in my family's affairs. He told me he also handled Uncle Sid's affairs, together with the galactic mining operation's legal matters. I listened with interest.

"Your father left you everything, apart from a few personal effects he has willed to your uncle. You are now a half-owner of the Eagle's Nest hideaway in the Eagle Mountains. Your uncle owns the other half."

This inheritance was not new knowledge to me.

Callas continued. "You inherit his apartment, but because of The Administration's regulations you may only personally live in it when you reach a level-one status."

With my job in space I would not need to live in the apartment so this news did not cause concern.

"I will arrange to sell it as soon as we have moved the personal effects," I said.

"That would be perfectly fine—I can handle this for you if you want—we just need to settle on a price. An important issue is the financial credit his estate will provide. It is reasonably substantial."

The estate held no interest for me in the past but with latest developments it would be expedient for me to smarten up and obtain an assessment of my net worth. I would need to take some time to find out more about the world stock market and make some wise investments. The present investment strategy, according to Callas, performed well for the time being but the future required some planning.

"There is also the question of intellectual property. Your father invested a great deal of his own time into past discoveries and the WGF will try to claim all of it as their property."

"How can we get by that? It's a legal matter most companies tie up tighter than their wage increments," I said.

"Your father was a careful man. He has logged all the time spent on every one of his discoveries. In particular, the recent longevity research—he called it the A-Mortal Gene—is outside the official location and time allocated for normal working hours."

"But the directors claim to have been working in unison with him. One of the secretaries said she could actually help me with a file on all the pre-work."

"The pre-work, they are talking about, is mostly common knowledge made in previous discoveries and would be needed for advancement—principally, for any further discovery in longevity."

The enormity of the problem hacked its way into my awareness.

"So, you are saying they are going to steal this new discovery and claim it as their own, using the intellectual property law?"

Callas dropped his chin. "Not only will they steal the property rights but it's possible someone will try to cash-in on it. There could be billions of credits involved in developing the finished product for commercial sale."

It all fell into place. The discovery of a genetic code enhancement, which gave humans a much longer lifespan, would be a bonanza for any entrepreneur.

"Your father's last contact with me came two days before his death—his last request—to encourage you to use some of your inheritance to upgrade your education to a level-one in bio-molecular and neurological studies and continue on with the work."

The old sensation of anger wanted to raise its head but I cut it off. I now understood the stakes. Did I want to complicate my life, by taking over the baton from my dad? This answer still remained shrouded in uncertainty.

The lawyer cocked his head to one side and smiled.

"He told me about the info-vial—you will know where to find it. You need to be extremely vigilant if you decide to follow up on this as there are those who would want to get their hands on it. Of course, it's your life, so whatever you decide is your business, but if you can drop in at my offices, perhaps tomorrow, or sometime before spacing out to the asteroid belt—"

"Yes, I'll do that," I said. "There are things that probably need my signature."

Callas shook my hand and turned his attention to the refreshment table. My mind reflected on the conversation, with immediate attention paid to the intellectual property. A crucial asset, once my father's personal property, now belonged to his estate and as the estate's main beneficiary, its contents had been ceded to me.

"A half-credit for you thoughts?" Freda asked.

"It's nothing—the lawyer wanted to inform me regarding my dad's estate. I need to meet with him before I return to the belt."

Uncle Sid came to stand next to Freda. "I see you chatted with our Mr. Callas?"

"Yeah, nice fellow, actually—said he remembers me as a small boy, before mom died."

Sid grinned and swirled the cafteen in his mug. "I could tell you many stories about when you were a small boy."

Changing the subject, I asked, "When are we going to Eagle's Nest? I need to sign papers at the lawyer's office."

Uncle Sid looked at Freda. "When?"

"You need to call the Andromeda tonight—Gary Pearson needs to confer with you about something. I have a few things to attend to in the morning and Beckett needs to sign papers. I say we stay one more night at the Orion and then leave for Eagle's Nest on the first."

"Sounds fine to me—okay with you, Beckett?"

I agreed. "Let's get out of here—I need a drink."

We took the escalator to the lawyer's office, about two blocks from the hotel, and I dispensed signatures on several legal documents.

On the way back to the Orion, Freda reminded me of the unopened bottle of whiskey and suggested we grab it for a pre-dinner drink. In complete agreement with the suggestion, I told her and Uncle Sid we could meet downstairs in the lounge to drink a final salute to my late father.

It would seem my attitude to the past tenuous relationship deserved a welcome change. I no longer felt a knot in my stomach regarding my Dad, and the memory of his parental neglect morphed into a father who took his vocation too seriously.

My anger evaporated, but guilt replaced it. The hard-ass attitude held far too long needed a new approach—a change I felt comfortable with.

On arrival at the Orion, Uncle Sid and Freda made straight for their rooms while I decided to use the ablution chamber downstairs. Half an hour still remained before my father's final salute and I thought it a great idea to slip into the bar and lay a good foundation.

While I stood at the urinal, a person came in to use the hand-sanitizer, and inserted his hands into the driers. I took no notice of the individual and concentrated on the business at hand. I finished up and walked toward the entrance. The door opened and another man barged into me. I stepped back and felt a sharp pain in the back of my head.

∞∞

Sixteen

A Severe Beating

I woke to unfamiliar surroundings, strapped to a chair. Pin-stripe's familiar voice filtered through the noise of the runaway buzz-saw in my head which throbbed with a vicious intent. Warm blood trickled down my neck from a head-wound, somewhere behind my left ear. Back at the hotel, I remembered a person at the washroom door before a heavy blow, on the back of my head, plunged everything into darkness.

"So, Mr. Conroy. We meet again under slightly different circumstances."

Still dazed, I tried to get up from the chair but straps restrained all my movement.

"What do you want with me?"

"Oh, I'm sure you must have realized what we're after from our previous meeting."

"I haven't a clue what you're talking about." The patronizing tone in his voice grated on me.

"Come now, Mr. Conroy! You must remember what your father—sorry, your late father—asked you to do?"

"What he asked of me has nothing to do with you two shitheads."

Pin-stripe's ugly partner, turned to look at him. "Shall I jog his memory?"

Pin-stripe smiled and I guessed at his intentions. A blow from a rubber cudgel caught the bridge of my nose and a splatter of blood decorated the front of my nano-suit.

Like a trained pit bull Ugly-one looked to his master, who indulged him with a nod.

The second blow caught my jaw and almost dislodged a bottom molar. Warm blood filtered into my mouth and down my throat, which caused me to choke and throw up. To the amusement of Ugly-one I spat the blood onto the floor and he hit me again. This time the blow fell above my left eye which swelled like a balloon.

I glared at Pin-stripe defiantly. "You can beat me all you fucking want, but I don't have anything for you."

Due to the swelling of my nose and the blood in my mouth, the words sounded as though I spoke with a mouth full of porridge. Ugly-one raised his arm again to strike another blow but Pin-stripe restrained his hand.

"Mr. Conroy—save yourself a lot of trouble and just tell us where the info-vial is."

"I haven't had time to work it out yet."

Ugly-one laughed out allowed. "He's not going to tell us. Let's just do the memory sweep."

Pete nodded and they attached soft pads to my each of my temples. The pads, joined to a device with several strobe lights, felt cold and wet against my skin. This particular innovation appeared in the omninet international space magazine and I remembered a photo of it—a memory sweeper.

Pin-stripe twiddled around with the device and an electrical field passed through my mind like a bolt of lightning. Waves of electrical noise jammed all other sound until I passed out. My final thought centered on one consolation—not enough information within my active memory to pinpoint a specific place for the clue. From what I remembered of the article in the space magazine, the memory sweeper could not gain access to long-term memories.

Ten minutes later I woke to the persistent throb in my head and Pin-stripe stood over me like the ancient Statue of Liberty.

"It seems hard to believe you haven't actually worked on that riddle your father left you."

My answer must have sounded absurd. "No time—I'm not keen to get involved."

Ugly-one's voice chirped from behind. "Don't talk bullshit, Conroy!"

Pin-stripe looked dubious. "There are billions of credits to be made. Why would you not be interested?"

"My father and I never got along."

Pin-stripe turned to his cohort. "Listen to this fucking drivel—maybe you should smack him again."

He moved aside to allow Ugly-one room to swing the cudgel. My stomach wanted to heave.

There seemed little I could do to prevent these two morons from bludgeoning me to death. Then a thought came—without me they would have no means of working out the clue.

"Stop! I'll make a deal with you," I shouted.

Ugly-one stopped mid-swing and the cudgel bruised my shoulder. He looked at Pin-stripe, who motioned for him to step back.

"Let's hear what he has to say."

Relieved beyond measure, my mind worked overtime to think of what I could offer them. These two idiots operated on the instructions of the 'prominent member of society', Pin-stripe referred to in our first confrontation and it would be better for me to speak with him.

"If you kill me, you have nothing. I'll make a deal, but not with you—I will speak to the scumbag who gives your orders."

A moment's silence followed. They glanced at each other and Pin-stripe knelt down, his eyes inches from mine.

"Let's get this straight, Conroy. If we kill you, fair enough, we will have nothing. If you want to speak to the boss-man it can be arranged—but it won't stop us from beating your ass a little more."

"When do I get to speak to him?"

Pin-stripe straightened and took a step backward.

"Give him one or two more—I need to make a quick call. Make sure he'll be able to talk."

Ugly-one grinned, threw the cudgel down and stepped forward with both fists raised in the stance of a boxer about to enter a brawl. He let go two short punches, one on each side of my face which caused my head to bobble like a gymnasium speed ball. He then finished off with a shot to the solar-plexus.

For a minute or two, breathing became almost impossible and I faltered in a semiconscious state as my system went into shock. My entire body collapsed into an uncontrollable fit of the shakes as I sat, still strapped into the chair.

The moment before darkness overtook me, I watched Ugly-one take a step back to survey his handy-work.

∞∞

Seventeen

That Prominent Member of Society

The cold water induced consciousness and with a shake of the head came partial lucidity. The movement caused serious pain and my eyes opened enough to see several human shapes before me. The straps still held me to the chair.

Pin-stripe stooped to gaze with an attitude of belligerence.

"Someone has come to talk to you, Conroy. You'd better not be fucking with us about making a deal."

I spat out more blood. With swollen lips and a tongue twice its normal size, my speech sounded abnormal, however, I needed to make a case for my continued mortality. Pin-stripe moved aside and a familiar face peered at me, with interest.

The sallow skin, long pointed nose and bushy eyebrows, still etched into my memory from our recent visit to the WGF, gave the visitor away—Dr. Nassir.

His voice flowed like viscus oil, the tone friendly, but serious.

"I see my men have done quite a number on you, Beckett."

Ugly-one brought a chair for him to sit on. Nassir's eyes never left mine for one moment. We stared at each other for a few brief seconds before I answered.

"Why am I not surprised to see you here, Nassir?"

He ignored the statement. "What's this deal you want to make?"

"I would not normally make deals with scumbags like you. You are nothing more than a leach, hoping to gain fame and fortune from the work of others."

"Spare me the morality lecture, Beckett, and get to the point, before I turn my men loose on you again."

For fear that the shitheads might beat me to death I capitulated.

"Okay. You win, Nassir—here is my proposal—give me until the fourth of July to come up with the whereabouts of the vial. The riddle I have to solve is something stemming from the very distant past. I have to work it out."

Dr. Nassir regarded my proposal with suspicion. "And then—"

"Then, we talk about sharing the prize."

He smirked and the friendly tone disappeared.

"Listen to me, Conroy. The only deal I am prepared to make with you doesn't include sharing anything."

My window of salvation frosted over. "What exactly do you mean?"

"Finding the info-vial and turning it over to me is the only thing standing between you and the well-being of someone close to you."

Nassir's words clouded over any patch of blue sky there might have been.

"Who are you talking about?"

Nassir stood and walked around the chair and placed his hands on the backrest.

"I am a well-organized individual. I foresee the possibilities and take care of the necessary."

He turned and motioned to Ugly-one. "While you were unconscious, my man stole away and took care of your friend."

The discussion took on a more ominous tone.

"My friend? Who are you talking about?"

"I'm talking about your girlfriend, Miss Banning."

Fear crowded out any hope of an equal-term deal with these lowlifes. The thought of Freda, subjected to the torturous hand of the ugly monster on Nassir's pay role, brought me to the point of tears.

"If he's harmed her in anyway, I swear, I'll kill him."

The venom with which I expressed the words caused all three men to laugh.

"Don't you worry about a thing, Beckett. She's safe—for now—as long as you play ball with us."

Stunned by his words I could not think of how to counter his plan but decided to test his resolve.

"You're a ruthless bastard, Nassir. How do I know you are telling the truth?"

He held my intensive gaze. "We are going to release you now. When you get back to the Orion you may ask your uncle. He witnessed my man's little escapade in the hallway, outside Miss Banning's room."

"You better not have harmed either of them, you asshole, because if I ever get my hands on you—"

Nassir made a hand-motion—a signal for Ugly-one to release me. The shithead worked on the buckles of the straps that held me to the chair and then gave it a vicious kick which caused me to topple over sideways. In a final act of barbarism, while I lay helpless on the floor, he stomped his boot on the side of my face.

Nassir confirmed his demand. "You have until the fourth of July, Conroy—get me the vial and your girlfriend will be released, unharmed."

Again I experienced excruciating pain and passed out.

*

I awoke with terrible head pain. For the enemy, my imagination ranged from scrotum emasculation to full genital removal. The ugly shithead, in particular, would be singled out for very special treatment in the near future. And as for that asshole of a doctor—.

A vision of Freda's pretty face dispelled my speculative brood and the two most important issues came to mind—the need to find her location, plus the whereabouts of the info-vial. Vengeance could wait.

The way back to the Orion presented some difficulties. The escalators, planned on a grid system, tested my confused mind but after a while I found the right direction. When I arrived at the Orion Uncle Sid sat in the bar-lounge, with a drink in hand and a worried look.

A glance at my face brought a look of horror to the president commander's face.

"Good Lord! What on earth did they do to you—are you okay?"

A red mark under his left eye told its own story. I explained what had taken place.

"I know they've taken Freda—did they hurt either of you?" I asked.

"I got clipped under the eye by the rough-neck who beat you up, but I'm okay. Fortunately he didn't hurt Freda. Nassir has over-stepped the mark by taking her."

I needed to clean up and address my injuries so we decided to talk in my room, the ablution chamber of which contained a cabinet, with basic bathroom requirements and some medical supplies. Once in the room, Happydoo stepped out of the charge booth and observed my condition.

'Did you have a fall, Master Beckett?'

Uncle Sid grabbed a wet swab out of the cabinet and wiped the congealed blood from my nose and face while he told us what happened to Freda.

"I was standing, talking to Freda outside her room in the hallway, when this man stepped out of the verticap. He grabbed her by the arm—I tried to stop him, but he punched me under the eye, as you can see."

"Did he say anything to you?" I asked.

"Yes, he did. Freda struggled but he injected her with some sort of sedative to make her compliant, then he told me to wait for you. He said not to go to the police—you would explain everything."

Happydoo looked thoughtful and responded. *'Do you think I should contact the police, Master Beckett?'*

Androids have a built in omninet communication system, connected by dozens of overhead satellites. It would be a simple matter for it to make immediate contact with the police, but the thought of Freda, in Nassir's possession, terrified the life out of me.

"No, Happydoo. We would be placing Miss Freda's life in imminent danger by doing that. What we must do is work on finding the info-vial and the location of her imprisonment."

Uncle Sid applied some ointment from the cabinet to my swollen eye. "I'm really concerned as to what they'll do to Freda. I am going to contact the Andromeda and let them know we won't be coming back on the fourth as originally planned."

"Not to be taken as a consolation, but Nassir said they would not harm her providing I produce the info-vial," I added.

Uncle Sid looked doubtfully. "Have you been able to work on the clue—do you know where the vial is?"

"I need to think on it tonight—I have a gut feel it will be in the vicinity of Eagle's Nest. Tomorrow I have a meeting with Carla Jensen at 0900 hours."

'Hopefully Miss Jensen could provide some information on its location, Master Sidney,' said Happydoo.

A little bent out of shape by the day's events, I needed sleep.

"I wouldn't bank on it but I'm confident I will work it out—one way or another. I'm heading for bed."

Uncle Sid added, "You must be feeling awful. I think the swellings will go down quickly."

He held up a tube taken from the medical assortment. "This anti-swell lotion is excellent stuff."

∞∞

Eighteen

Meeting with Carla

The first rays of sunlight diffused through the overhead dome and into my bedroom as I drifted out of the arms of Morpheus.

I checked the time—0750 hours—perfect. My head felt like a bag stuffed with broken concrete pieces and though the swellings appeared to have subsided, the skin still felt tender to the touch —a testimony to the anti-swell lotion.

The previous evening a search for the info-vial's location took me about ten minutes, before a much welcomed sleep overwhelmed me. The answer surfaced after a nostalgic walk down memory lane to revisit the earlier years of my life. The content of the clue seemed familiar and connected to the many excursions my father and I undertook at our hideaway-vacation home in the Eagle Mountains. With the knowledge of the info-vial's location, a nervous apprehension prevailed for Freda's safe return. I knew the responsibility lay on my shoulders.

Morning ablutions commanded my attention for ten minutes, followed by the selection of a sport-suit coverall from the auto-dress fabricator.

Happydoo released himself from the charge booth and waited to inspect my injuries, with his usual brand of techno-induced humor. *'Your face has been greatly improved by the beating, Master Beckett.'*

"Thanks, Happydoo. It's perhaps a good thing androids are programmed to never harm a human—I might have asked you to beat me up occasionally."

The android repeated his little action of knuckle-bite mirth and responded, *'In that case I would have been happy to do it for you, Master Beckett.'*

Not used to the services of a valet the android's presence changed the ambience of my normal routine. None of the human staff aboard the Andromeda retained them and with the exception of several Mine supervisory jobs, the majority of AI's were bots.

With regard to Happydoo, a question presented itself.

"You were actually the one to plant the vial in some secret place?"

'That is true, Master Beckett, however, as Master Padraig said—he removed the location from my memory to protect its whereabouts.'

I considered Happydoo's answer for a moment. "So, you have absolutely no idea where it is?"

'Not really, Master Beckett, however—one thing not yet considered is the GPS record before the day of Master Padraig's murder. This record lies within a restricted area of my passive memory.'

"Are you able to access the passive memory?"

'I believe so, Master Beckett—give me a moment.'

Muted electronic sounds emanated from the android's head as it attempted to locate the

GPS record within the passive memory of the processor. In a flash the answer came.

'The vial is close to the Eagle's Nest, hideaway. I have only basic coordinates but not the exact location, Master Beckett.'

"Thank you, Happydoo. You have just confirmed the result of my search before falling asleep last night."

'I am happy to have been of service, Master Beckett.'

With the main location pinned down, I turned to look in an adjacent wall mirror. A pang of trepidation flooded my thoughts, to bring the seriousness of our situation to mind—Freda! The thought of her anguish made me feel guilty in retrospect of my attempt at early morning levity.

This sentiment might be lost on the likes of Happydoo so I didn't mention it. Despite the reflection, there appeared to be no denial of excitement, spawned by the potential meeting with Carla.

The woman's beauty and elegance projected the natural poise of royalty, a refined and sophisticated grace, retained only by those of high breeding. Constant thoughts and impressions of our first two meetings, rendered my heart to a state of pliable putty. I wanted to get to know her.

Uncle Sid did not answer the ID-comm to his room, so I assumed he might be downstairs in the foyer. At 0850 hours, Happydoo accompanied me to the Orion's entrance—no sign of Uncle Sid. It seemed a little odd but maybe he overslept and did not hear the comm. I decided to proceed and fill him in later.

The early-morning rush appeared to have subsided. Nick's Cafteen House could seat about thirty people and to find it almost empty came as a huge relief. Choosing a lone table at the back, with the hope of privacy, I sat where I could see the door. Happydoo parked himself opposite and we waited for Carla to arrive.

Five minutes later she entered, dressed in a gorgeous tight-fit, nano-suit. The long, blonde hair swept back from the high forehead, cascaded like a waterfall over her shoulders and prominent breasts strained against the tight fabric of the suit. I remained captivated by the emerald-colored eyes as they caught my own in a hypnotic embrace.

Happydoo stood and offered her his seat while I stared, mesmerized. She smiled and offered me a dainty hand which turned out to have a strong grip, unlike the touch I remembered at the memorial. A sudden self-consciousness with regard to my disfigured face, spoilt the moment for me.

"What on Earth happened to you?" she asked.

"It's a long story—I won't bore you with the details."

Happydoo asked if he could order two mugs of cafteen on our behalf. I asked him to order me some yogatol and cam fruit for breakfast.

Carla declined the offer. "I'm an early riser and have already eaten, thanks."

The android went to place my order while Carla and I observed each other with interest.

"Please tell me what happened. I can assure you, I'll not be bored."

My smile in response proved a little too much for my facial injuries and I winced. My answer fell short of the whole truth.

"I was accosted by two men last night."

"Accosted? They certainly did a number on you," she said.

Desperate to change the subject, it occurred that I knew very little about this woman. She worked for the WGF and therefore might be in cahoots with the infamous Dr. Nassir.

"Do you enjoy working at the WGF?"

"Yes, it's not a bad place to work. I did some admin work for your late father and kept a record of his research."

"How well do you know Dr. Nassir?"

She searched my face for a hint of emotion and a lapse of silence ensued in which my heart skipped a beat.

"My honest opinion?"

"Yes. Give me your impression—I mean as a coworker, a friend, a member of the foundation?"

Carla looked at her hands, and then her gaze shifted to Happydoo.

He apologized for the interruption, placed the food with the mug of cafteen in front of me and took an adjacent seat. The android looked first at me and then at her, in expectation.

"Thank you, Happydoo." My appreciation for the android's consideration would be answered in the usual way.

'I am happy to do it for you, Master Beckett.'

I turned my attention back to Carla.

"Your impressions?"

"Dr. Nassir, in my opinion, is a jerk."

I was surprised at her bluntness.

"He only thinks of himself. He is always making lewd comments behind my back and thinks I can't hear."

"Does he know you are here this morning?"

Carla frowned. "God, no! He would probably try to get me fired if he knew."

My relief must have shown. "So, you don't get on with him?"

"I tolerate him because it's part of my job. He is so far up Jameson's ass that it's difficult for me to say anything."

"How did you get along with my dad?"

"Your father always made me feel important. He worked very hard and often confided little frustrations about his work."

I cleared my throat. "You know, of course, about the genetic breakthrough?"

"Yes—the A-Mortal gene, he called it. I have brought you an info-vial on everything he recorded before going dark."

"Going dark?"

"Sorry. I meant he stopped officially recording progress."

"You knew he had continued in an unofficial capacity?"

"He told me as much. Dr. Nassir became over-interested in the work—searching through every record—demanding to know where the rest of the research was being kept."

"Did my father ever mention me?"

"Many times—he spoke of the wonderful times you and he spent at Eagle's Nest."

My thoughts for Carla took a new turn. She did not appear to have a sinister motive, other than to be of help to me and I doubted she could be in league with Nassir. In fact, my belief in her innocence rapidly morphed into a strong sensation of trust.

"What would you say if I told you the two men who assaulted me last night work directly for him?"

She shot me a startled glance. "One, tall, ugly and bald, the other dressed like a dandy?"

"You seem to know these two guys."

"They often visit Dr. Nassir—I'm not sure why—about some business or other."

My facial contortion gave my emotions away.

"After my colleagues and I arrived back at the hotel, from the memorial service, those two shitheads jumped me in the washroom. We ended up at an old deserted warehouse where the ugly one did his best to alter my looks."

Carla's eyes opened wide. "The bastards—I always thought they looked seedy."

"Our friend Nassir joined them after they had half beaten me to death—I said I would only make a deal with the dick pulling their strings."

"What sort of a deal did you discuss?"

"Nassir told me he wanted the info-vial my dad had mentioned so 'all' could benefit from the discovery."

Carla's eyes narrowed to mere slits. "I guess you must have agreed on something, since you're here to tell me the tale."

"I had little choice. Apart from abducting me they also took Uncle Sid's secretary, Freda Banning, as collateral. They have her holed up somewhere in the city."

"So, to save your uncle's secretary from a nasty outcome, you're being forced to hand over the final part of your dad's research?"

"It appears that way. I now know where it is, more or less."

Carla placed her hand over mine and stared into my eyes.

"You must be under so much stress—can I be of any assistance? I actually have the next three days off and I would love to help in whatever way I can."

My heart did a somersault and Happydoo took it as a cue to make a comment.

'I am sure Master Beckett would be happy to have you accompany us to Eagle's Nest, Miss Jenson.'

Carla's eyes held mine in expectation as I made a bad imitation of feigning my doubt. Her hand still lay on top of mine—she seemed oblivious of it and made no attempt to withdraw the gesture. The silent message transmitted to my ego like a noisy bell. With dry throat I stuttered my acceptance.

"Of course, we would be delighted to have you along.

"It's settled then. When will you be leaving? I need to pick up some necessities from my apartment. Will your uncle be accompanying us?"

"Yes, as far as I know—he's worried sick about Freda, as we all are. We missed him this morning. It's possible he may be trying to work out where they might be keeping her."

'Master Sidney knows many people in Quantum City, Master Beckett. He might be trying to corral information about Dr. Nassir's assets for a clue. It would not be surprising if he does not accompany us.'

I pursed my lips. "You may be right, Happydoo. I might suggest he stay here in the city while we go to Eagle's Nest. If any information concerning Freda's location arises, my uncle would be able to follow up on it immediately."

Another motive for not having Uncle Sid accompany us, lay in the alone time I would have with Carla.

"Pick up whatever you need and we will meet you in the foyer of the Orion at 1200 hours—would that be okay for you?"

"Excellent. I'll see you at 1200," she said.

Carla gave my hand a little squeeze and made to leave. I stood and almost knocked the table over in the process. We looked at each other for what seemed an eternity before she turned and with a cursory nod in Happydoo's direction, left Nick's.

My entire sensory system grappled with disbelief. The world, which seemed so bleak, took on a sudden change of fortune. Despite the challenge of the vial's discovery and the need to obtain Freda's release—Carla's presence suggested an amazing improvement in my position.

∞∞

Nineteen

Eagle's Nest

A trip to Eagle's Nest did not appeal to Uncle Sid. He maintained it would be better if he remained in Quantum City and followed up on any information he could find regarding Freda's location.

"I have contacted some of my old associates who are trying to accumulate information on Nassir. If we can pin down his building assets there may be a few leads to follow up on."

Uncle Sid seemed a little perturbed with regard to Carla's sudden inclusion but I ensured him she made it quite clear—Nassir did not register as her most favorite person.

"She brought an info-vial with all dad's research currently at the WGF. This is a huge risk for her."

"She may be pulling the wool over your eyes," he said.

"Maybe, but I will handle it if she is—besides, I think she could be quite helpful."

"Suit yourself, Beckett. Just find the vial and call me when you have it. I'm terrified they will harm Freda."

"I understand your concern, Uncle Sid. Happydoo and I will handle the vial situation from our end. May I borrow your cortex transmitter?"

Upstairs in my room, Happydoo treated himself to a quick charge in the booth which gave me time to freshen up and wash my face. The bluish-purple bruises around my eye and nose looked spectacular but showed a significant reduction in the swelling.

There would be no need for me to pack anything as the hideaway possessed an auto-dress fabricator and meal replicator. I decided to take the anti-swell lotion and some mouthwash, which I placed into a small travel case, which also contained the info-vial of WGF research Carla gave me.

At 1150 hours, Happydoo unplugged from the charger and we took the verticap to the foyer.

Carla waited for us, a backpack slung over her strong, slim shoulders and dressed in an outdoor coverall with hiking boots to match. She looked lovely, despite the drab color of the hiker's garb. Again, when I looked into those emerald eyes, my pulse raced like a runaway magnotrain.

The underground train system ran beneath the escalators. The trains, encased in a tube, ran on electromagnetic propulsion and could reach speeds of up to 3000 km per hour on longer hauls, between provinces. Within the metro-city area such speeds were not possible due to the short distances traveled between stops. The method of transport, however, served as the most inexpensive and quickest form for longer distances.

We sat encased in the protective seats and looked around at the other passengers. A small contingent of bots locked into special racks took up one end of the capsule and a few people scattered themselves around, seated in the available compression couches. Besides Happydoo, two other androids took up an AI rack near the door of the train. Our short trip would end at the Spaceport, where Uncle Sid kept an antigravity vehicle.

The antigravity hangers situated in a twenty-story building, accommodated ten thousand antigrav transporters of different types and sizes. The process of storage and selection operated on an automated system and worked by cerebral cortex transmission. Each hanger had a specific number and the vehicle delivery took only a matter of minutes.

I transmitted the antigrav and hanger codes, but because of high request volumes, a longer than usual time-lag ensued. After ten minutes the transporter arrived at the pickup platform and the delivery-mule deposited it onto the takeoff ramp. The usual standard, automated audio command followed:

Your transport has been serviced and all life support systems are in good working order. Caution: you have thirty seconds to embark and leave the ramp before retrieval is ordered.

I commanded the door of the vehicle to open and we jumped into the flight seats. Outside, a mist rose around the antigrav as the system fired up and the hanger hooks released to free the transporter for flight. I spoke the coordinates to the command computer.

The gravity restraint cancelled allowing the vehicle to rise and hover for a few seconds before it shot off with a sudden spurt of power.

Within seconds our transporter reached the standard operation height of two hundred meters and the immense power of the thrusters forced us back into our seats as the vehicle winged along at Mach two. The airport garage diminished in size and soon disappeared from our sight altogether as the vehicle scribed a wide arc over the sea. It then turned back toward land in response to the pro-grammed destination coordinates.

The radiation shield appeared to function with its normal efficiency and all systems showed positive for a safe flight. The onboard computer would guide the transporter straight to Eagle's Nest, the recreational cabin my father and Uncle Sid inherited from my grandfather. The hideaway, secluded under the overhang of a cliff, could not be reached overland.

The transporter would park itself on top of the cliff overhang, above the hideaway and remain on a pad in the open. Occupants of the Eagle's Nest accessed the accommodation through a vertical tunnel dug into the roof of the overhang.

From the main lounge the occupiers enjoyed a beautiful view through the cabin's front balcony windows. The hideaway could accommodate three families and boasted a meal-replicator plus an auto-dress fabricator. Water, pumped up to a holding tank from the valley below made the abode self-sufficient for long-term stays.

The antigrav landed on the pad in front of the hideaway's entrance in a cloud of dust and small stones. I commanded the computer to turn the thrusters off after which we disembarked the cockpit and scuttled into the entrance portal for the tunnel.

Carla and I took care not to expose ourselves to the dangerous rays of the sun while in transition from the antigrav to the verticap.

The latest update in regard to radiation exposure for the region brought with it an ominous warning of the Earth's failed ozone layer which protected us from radiation contamination.

The Aurora lights, now a constant occurrence, ranged over much of the planet to give spectacular lightshows throughout the night. No humans inhabited any areas near the poles anymore. The extreme conditions caused the total melt off of all glaciers and consequent rise in sea levels.

To conserve power and protect radiation from seeping through the main entrance, my dad installed a door of solid iron construction with a lead lining. The inbuilt combination lock could be activated by CCT command.

After I unlocked the door, we squashed into the small verticap and dropped through thirty meters of rock to arrive on the first level of the hideaway. A gravity stabilizer within the capsule interior, held our bodies in check for the brief two-second descent.

Carla and Happydoo stepped onto the polished marble floor of the sitting room and gazed around at the furnished area—all appeared to be in good order. I motioned Carla to check out the view from the large viewing-windows that faced the gorge.

Mesmerized, she stood transfixed and stared at the surrounding canyon walls and the valley in the far distance. Beyond, lay the magnificent plains of the Eagle Mountain National Park, no longer a tourist attraction due to the radiation factor. Because of the high, rocky walls, the gorge remained protected from much of the sun's harmful radiation. Despite the stunted nature of the shrubs and dry brown grass, a distinct impression of nature's freedom reigned over the scene.

"This is so beautiful," said Carla.

I stood beside her, close enough for her arm to touch mine—tingles of pleasure coursed through my body. My silence forced her to turn from the scenery, our eyes meeting for the briefest second before I averted my stare of awe. In a twinkle, I saw promise and commitment, as a hint of a smile appeared on her lips.

Happydoo chose this moment to intervene. *'Can we talk about the info-vial, Master Beckett?'*

My magic mirror shattered into a thousand shards.

"Shit, Happydoo—we've only just arrived—we were enjoying the beautiful scenery and a peaceful moment."

'My apologies, Master Beckett, but should we not retrieve the vial first? It will soon be dark.'

Carla could see my frustration and turned back to the scenery with a grin. She knew what caused my exasperation with the android which had nothing to do with our recent arrival.

My heavy sigh accompanied by a crestfallen look must have said it all for her. I caught her eye and she gave me a wink of assurance—we would continue our special moment later.

∞∞

Twenty

The Hideaway—Settling In

"Exactly what was the clue your father left for you," asked Carla.

I sat at the sitting room table and recited the first part of my dad's clue:

"In a time long ago, he died in a fall,
While looking for eggs in the nest—"

She waited in anticipation of my answer and I hesitated for a moment to gather my thoughts.

"When I was about six years old, my dad brought me here one weekend and we walked out into the valley. If you look out the window you will see it below. The sun's radiation factor was not as dangerous as it is today, but still, we wore large hats and long sleeved suits to protect our skin."

Carla interrupted. "I guess you went hunting for bird's nests and eggs."

I grinned at the innocence of her observation based on the clue.

"Not really. We were walking along the edge of the gorge, when I spotted an old track. It hadn't been used in many years. I let go of my dad's hand and ran along it, ignoring his shouts to be careful. The track followed along the base of the cliff overhang where there used to be a stream—only a dry bed by that time. I never saw it."

I Paused for effect in the hope Carla would tear her attention from the scenery. After a brief moment I succeeded and our eyes met.

Happydoo, once again, jumped in. *'What did you not see, Master Beckett?'*

"God, Happydoo—I'm about to tell you."

'My apologies, Master Beckett. I am happy to zip my lip and wait for your explanation.'

I didn't respond to the comment and continued with my story.

"I ran head-on into an old gravestone. My dad quickly followed up on my enquiry as to its purpose. A man in the nineteenth century had apparently been climbing in the cliffs overlooking the river's edge when he lost his footing and fell to his death. He had been searching for bird's nests."

Carla pulled up a chair and sat at the table. "You believe your father has hidden the vial at the old grave site?"

"The clue certainly fits the old story. The mention of 'a man dying while looking for eggs in a nest,' seems to correlate well. It's possible he has buried the vial where the grave stone lies."

'The coordinates of the GPS indicate this to be the area where I placed the vial. When do you intend going out to the gravesite, Master Beckett?'

"The journey down the gorge will take about two hours, plus another half-hour, or so, to the old river bed. It's a bit late to set out now—the sun will be down within three hours."

'If you prefer, Master Beckett, I would be happy to do the journey tomorrow morning while you and Miss Jenson relax here in the hideaway. The maximum length of time a human's skin may be exposed to the sun's rays is twenty minutes, before radiation damage takes place.'

"You make a good point, Happydoo. There are two protective suits in storage, however, you would be able to make the journey much faster."

'I would be happy to do it at my fastest possible pace, depending on the terrain, Master Beckett. You could program the route I should take, plus uploading a drawing of the site to my processor.'

The benefits of this suggestion came with an added bonus for me—more time alone with Carla.

"You could give us a visual of your journey as you travel—we can use the CCT to communicate."

The living room setup included an omni-holographic receiver platform which could receive visuals from all over the world. Happydoo's processor would be able to transmit his visual surroundings for the entire duration of the mission. Use of the CCT would make it possible for me to communicate with him and answer any questions he might come up with.

With this decision behind us the android, on my suggestion, parked itself in the charge-booth for a power-system rejuvenation, while Carla and I checked out the rest of the hideaway.

"Where will I be sleeping tonight?" she asked.

Six bedrooms formed three separate living quarters. Each living quarter possessed an ablution chamber, plus a private lounge for enhanced personal comfort. Different décor characterized each apartment but a common feature to all was the transparency of each wall that faced the gorge.

The cliff overhang ranged up and outward above the viewing wall. In years gone by we watched birds build their nests, many of which hung from fissures in the rocks. The increased radiation factor brought the eventual decimation of all wild avian life.

"This room is one of my favorites," I said. I led the way into the first apartment, close to the living room.

Carla followed like a child in Wonderland.

Her eyes widened in appreciation of the viewing-wall. "It's like standing outside on a balcony with no protective barrier—so beautiful." She stood against the clear graphene-glass wall and gazed across the valley below.

"Don't look down, if you have a fear of heights."

The room, built from the side of the cliff wall under the overhang, gave the occupants an impression of floating on air.

Carla placed her hands against the glass. "I love it! I could live here forever."

"It jointly belonged to Uncle Sid and my father, but since dad's passing, the half-share has reverted to me."

She turned as I came to stand at the viewing wall. "Living on a mining vessel can't be too much fun. Do you think you might decide to get an Earth-bound job now with your dad gone—you could spend so much more time here."

Her steady gaze gave me goose-bumps. "I might, it depends—"

"On what?"

I blushed. "On whether there's a reason for me to stay—I guess."

I moved closer to her; might this be the right time to test the waters? She must have sensed my ambitious thoughts and turned away, to stare out at the valley. This action sent a subtle message to my rising libido and I felt all my hopes dissolve in an instant.

"Would you like something to drink?" I asked.

"Sure—do you have any wine?"

"There's a fully programmed meal replicator available. It has a full range of alcoholic beverages."

"Dry, white, for me, please. Can I take it this will be my room?"

"Be my guest," I answered.

The evening passed with little opportunity for me to close in on my dream to make love to Carla. One lesson learned through my years of dating women: they telegraphed their need to receive a man's close attention when they felt good and ready. A man should never reveal a strong desire to get woman into his bed—this creates an atmosphere of concern as to the powers of her womanly charms, because most women expect that sex is all the man wants. This gives him a measure of control. He must, of course, show interest, yet temper it with restraint.

We watched the World News on the holographic platform and made small talk for the remainder of the evening. Carla yawned and stretched out her long, slim legs.

"I think its time for me to turn in. What time will you send the android to find the vial, tomorrow?"

"I'll be up around 0800. It will take him a good four hours to get there and back—we don't know how long it will take him to find it."

My voice must have displayed some symptoms of disappointment at the lack of a signal from her, despite my efforts to show great interest, accompanied by maximum restraint. I guessed my psychology had become seriously screwed up or she suffered a bad experience in the past at the hands of a suitor. Whatever the reason it appeared certain my night would be spent in my own bed.

Carla moved over to the viewing window and stood stared out into the darkness. In the distance, the heavens glowed with the Aurora Borealis and spanned the full scope of the night sky. I came over to share the sight. To my amazement she leaned against me and allowed her head to rest on my shoulder.

Bewildered, my response was a little slow. Maybe my street-smart psychology worked and an excitement, amongst other things, rose up.

With an arm draped around her shoulders, I turned her to face me and allowed the olfaction of subtle and delightful perfume to permeate my senses. With eyes shut she raised her chin and parted lips in an invition to kiss her. My restraint vanished in an instant.

Hungrily in search of fulfilment our bodies locked in a sensual embrace and eternity seemed too short for me—but it appears even eternity comes to an end.

Carla, with a sudden movement, broke off the engagement and looked up at me—a tear welled out of one eye. "I'm sorry, Beckett—I shouldn't have—I can't—."

With a turn of shoulders and sudden retraction of arms, she slipped away and ran along the hallway to her room. All my hopes for the encounter drained away like emotional rainwater to disappear down a culvert of lost dreams.

I Heard the 'fizz' of her room's entrance force field activation, which announced the end of my quest for love. It brought a sense of despair felt only by the sensually bereaved. There remained nothing more for me to do but spend the night in confused thought and restless slumber. Where did I fail?

∞∞

Twenty-One

Mission Disrupted

At 0800 in the morning, Happydoo with CCT communication and a compact, foldable shovel in hand, took his leave of the hideaway. The holographic receiver-platform in the main living room, set up to receive a full view of the mission's progress as seen through the android's nano-camera eyes, provided us with his mission's progress.

With breakfast selected from the food-replicator, I sat at the viewing-wall and stared along the valley at Happydoo. His progress, after a steep descent down the cliff to the mountain's base, ensued with rapid efficiency.

I still awaited Carla's appearance for breakfast. The course of the night spent in an attempt to figure out a reason for my failure, came up with one assumption—it could not have been anything said or done on my behalf. Some bad experience in her past, a painful memory perhaps, hindered her pursuit of a relationship.

My hope hinged on a heart-to-heart conversation, to explore any possibility that out futures might have, to become entwined.

An hour later she traipsed into the living room and stifled a yawn. A low-key anger posited in my thoughts but the sight of her gladdened my heart to no end. We looked at each other for several seconds before she sat and said, "Can we talk about last night?"

"Gladly."

"It had nothing to do with anything you said or did."

My heart leapt with relief. "I am very glad to hear that."

Carla smiled and then became serious. "My husband died two years ago, and I'm still trying to salvage my life."

"I am very sorry for your loss—can you tell me how it happened?"

"He worked for the New World Earth Intelligence Agency and died in a shootout with a group of individuals trying to subvert The Administration."

"It must have been an awful shock for you."

My eye strayed to the holographic platform. Happydoo continued to make good progress toward the site of the old grave.

Carla nodded. "Every day gets better, but the pain of grief still lingers."

"Is there anything I can do to ease your pain?"

She leaned forward and looked straight into my eyes. "Just be patient with me, Beckett. I am attracted to you, but my heart is still mending—I need to learn to trust in love again."

"I understand. I feel an attraction too—I have never felt this way about anyone, but believe me, there's no pressure."

She smiled and reached across the table to take my hand. A sense of loss flooded my feelings, but the feel of her fingers in mine inspired a hope within me. She turned her attention to the receiver platform. "I see Happydoo is making great progress down there in the valley. How much longer 'til he reaches the gravesite?"

"About another forty minutes should do it. When he gets there, it might take a while to dig up the target area."

I continued to watch the transmission while Carla ordered her breakfast from the replicator.

She brought her meal to the table and sat. "Tell me more about your relationship with your father."

The sad details of my childhood unfolded while she listened. At first I felt a little guilty at the venom still present, but as the story began to evolve, I felt a greater measure of respect for my dad's achievements. My explanation reached the point where I gained employment on the Androm-eda and I received the awful news of my father's death.

Carla waited for me to run dry.

"I really liked your dad. He worked with a passion to find genetic breakthroughs—he provid-ed a distinct direction for the WGF to follow. No one else could stand toe-to-toe with him when it came to effort and leadership. Most of his col-leagues viewed him as a kind of hero."

Her words made a huge impression on me. This posed a different image of my father—one I never considered in previous times, but it all made sense now.

For a moment we listened in silence to Happydoo's footfalls as he trudged onward to the site. On the path ahead of him, through the sun-burned, knee-high grass a gravestone came into view.

Excitedly, I leaned forward. "There it is—the old grave."

Happydoo's voice boomed from within the hologram. *'I have arrived, Master Beckett. The site is very overgrown but it won't be a problem. I will start digging.'*

"Be careful, Happydoo—the info-vial should be in some sort of metal box—you wouldn't want to break it and destroy the information."

'I am happy to be very careful, Master Beckett.'

The android unfolded the compact shovel and made ready to dig at the base of the grave-stone. A heap of reddish, brown soil piled up on the one side under his efforts. We watched with excitement, but then the unexpected happened—the hologram disappeared from the receiver platform and the transmission ended without warning.

"What the hell—" I exclaimed.

Before I could say any more the video came back on for a few brief seconds. While it remained up Carla and I could see the cause of the problem. Before the transmission disappeared altogether, three suited forms approached Happydoo's position—one of them fired a weapon at the android's head.

∞∞

Twenty-Two

A Nasty Surprise

Carla and I identified the weapon used by the suited men, to fire upon Happydoo—an electromagnetic signal disrupter.

My response came with instantaneous venom. "It has to be those two shitheads again."

Carla countered my outburst. "I'm not so sure—I saw three people, not two."

After some thought, we agreed the extra person might be the 'prominent citizen' himself, Nassir.

My anger boiled over. "The swine couldn't live up to his side of the deal. By his own words, I had until the fourth of July to come up with the info-vial."

We needed to come up with a plan. To stay in the hideaway didn't seem a viable option, and I feared for the android's safety. Carla grabbed her backpack—I armed myself with a stun-ray laser my father kept in the locker of the storage unit, beneath the bedrooms.

If we maintained the element of surprise we should be able to immobilize one or more of the assailants, however, we needed to make it to the site before they left.

Carla and I reached the base of the mountain in good time. The hideaway, built into a section of the Eagle Mountains and encompassed by high cliffs on each side, gave some protection to the valley. The going became easier as the steep gradient fell away to more level ground and we moved across the floor of the gorge, to gain the path that ran along the valley.

Many memories from my past life flooded back, but I forced these out of my mind and we lengthened the gait of our strides, to improve the progress.

The suits, made of a radiation resistant, lightweight material, did a great job of skin protection but heat soon became a problem and I could feel the flow of perspiration down my legs. Carla wore the outfit my mother wore for a few short years, before her death—it seemed a good fit. The backpack bounced around on its straps as she loped along, its presence a mystery to me, but she wanted to bring it so I didn't question the decision.

There appeared to be no signs of the enemy's transportation, but it could have been parked anywhere in close proximity. The mountains provided dozens of places where an anrtigrav could land and be hidden from sight. With my thoughts focused on Happydoo's welfare I wondered how they knew the android would be in search of the vial.

The end of the valley loomed and we felt encouraged to pick up the tempo. Carla's level of fitness impressed me as she maintained the pace and never once fell behind. The path veered off to the left, close to the cliff face and for a while, heat from the sun's rays radiated off the cliff wall, to raise the temperature in the suits to an almost unbearable level. The sudden appearance of a figure, from behind a rocky crevice, stopped us in our tracks. The person, dressed in an anti-radiation suit, stepped onto the path in front of me.

Panicked into action I raised the stun gun and fired a beam but missed the assailant by a narrow margin. A voice cried out: "Drop your weapon, Conroy—we have you surrounded."

The tone of menace raised the hair on the back of my neck. In periphery vision, I saw someone to our right, jump out from behind a large rock. To the left, another suited form emerged out of the cliff face shadows. All three carried laser weapons, which left us with limited options.

I dropped the stun-gun and hoisted my hands into the air. Carla did the same, as one of the assailants checked me for concealed weapons.

My surprise turned to anger. "Who are you people?"

The man who addressed me kept the laser pointed at my chest. "I work for WGF security. We have been on the trail of Miss Jenson for illegally stealing classified intellectual property."

"Stealing?" My voice sounded strangulated. "You can't be serious—if you're talking about the info-vial she gave me yesterday, you are greatly mistaken. The so-called intellectual property belongs to my late father."

Carla remained silent, but I decided to stand up for our interests and in a show of bravado, dropped my hands and pushed the man away from me. As large as a tree trunk, he must have weighed at least 110 kg, which placed the advantage in his court. In one motion he retaliated and I found myself spread-eagled on the hard ground. Mister Tree-trunk then placed a huge boot on my chest and taunted me to try again.

The third person in the party grabbed Carla's backpack and pushed her to the ground. She did not offer any resistance but lay still, while he frisked her.

He opened the pack, gave a low whistle and picked out two items, to hold up in front of his face. "This is interesting."

A compact laser weapon and a leather badge holder. "Our little chick isn't really who she made herself out to be."

He threw the badge holder to the man who had initially addressed me.

"Hmmm, I see what you mean," he said.

He moved over to where Carla lay but kept the laser pointed at my chest.

"This complicates things. I'll need to talk to Jameson."

He turned his attention back to me and nodded to Tree-trunk who lifted his boot and took a step back.

"Get on your feet, Mr. Conroy and don't try anything stupid—We won't be so kind to you the next time."

I gathered my confused thoughts together and glanced at Carla, while the third member of the party helped her to stand. She remained calm and showed no signs of fear.

What did the leader's words mean? I wanted to ask her but this would not be possible under the present circumstances. The three men marched us toward the gravesite and my mind turned to Happydoo. I hoped his processor could still function.

The valley widened as we followed the cliff wall toward the area of the old, dry river bed. Soon the gravesite could be seen with the two heaps of soil on either side of the hole.

I could see the still form of Happydoo, face-down in the short, brown grass. He looked intact.

The WGF security team took no notice of him which begged my question. "Did you destroy the android's processor?"

The leader glanced at Happydoo. "It's only a machine, but to answer your question—no."

I felt an immense sense of relief.

"So where's the vial, Mr. Conroy?"

My surprise registered like an ancient seismograph. "You didn't find it in the grave?"

"Would I be asking you if we had?"

I felt dumfounded. The theory about my dad's riddle must have been incorrect and yet, everything about the clue, pointed to the gravesite. My dad's words rattled through my thoughts again like a rollercoaster.

'In a time long ago he died in a fall while looking for eggs in the nest—the vial is important, but in the end, your valet will pass the test.'

These sentences blurred together—something didn't seem right about my original analyses.

"I need to think about it. I really thought the vial was buried in the area of the grave."

"You had better think quickly—we don't have all day."

My anger flared again. "What makes you think I would tell you?"

"The life of your pretty little girlfriend depends on it. We don't mean you any harm, Mr. Conroy, but Dr. Jameson, my employer, says your father stole the discovery. In working for the foundation the information becomes the property of the WGF and not that of the discoverer."

"Do you have a name?" I asked.

The man stared at me for a long moment. "Sergeant Lapinski."

"Do you think Jameson has no plans to exploit this discovery?" I asked.

Lapinski looked thoughtful. "I don't really give a shit—he pays my salary."

The Sergeant made his point. His role did not include human ethics. An idea to strike a bargain with Jameson entered my mind. My knowledge of the vial's locality played a huge role in my preservation, but once they retrieved it, there would be no guarantees. I needed to buy some time.

"I must go over the clue my dad left and think about it."

"I can give you half an hour, but no more." Turning to the other two men he said, "Watch them closely. I'll be back in thirty."

∞∞

Twenty-Three

Retrieving the Info-Vial

Lapinski strode off, to make his way along the riverbed toward a section of mountain I knew well, from my childhood. Farther on an embankment of rock hid an open area of flat ground, a semi-circular enclave, carved out by a billion years of erosion. A transporter could be hidden there. The conversation earlier—Lapinski mentioned the need to talk with his boss—confirmed the reason for this present respite in our dire circumstances.

Carla looked at me through the visor of her suit's headgear. Her stare conveyed a hint of guilt, which I took to be a confession. In our discussion over breakfast she had hidden something from me. What could be so terrible that it warranted the omission?

My thoughts reverted back to the clue. The vial must be hidden here somewhere, but even if I knew the exact location, would it be in my best interests to hand it over to the WGF? On further deliberation I weighed up the importance of the vial against Carla's life. Would Lapinski harm her? To hand over the information might be my only option—but where did Happydoo place it?

I looked up at the cliff face to see several protrusions within reach of a good rock climber. A bush on one of the ledges, caught my eye. The clue mentioned: *bird's nests* and *climbing—my valet will pass the test*. It all fell into place.

High up on the cliff face, where the birds used to have their nests, might be a possible place for the vial's location. To find it would mean a precarious climb for someone. The ledge where the ancient egg-seeker clawed his way along and slipped, presented the best possible venue for an object like the vial, to be placed.

It made perfect sense for my dad to use the android to make the precarious deposit—Happydoo could outperform the most experienced of human rock climbers. Armed with this hope I felt better about our present situation.

It now became urgent to talk with Carla but when I tried to move closer to her, Tree-trunk moved between us and motioned me back to my allocated spot of dirty, brown grass.

There remained no option but to wait for the sergeant's return. I decided not to gamble with Carla's life. If the vial's discovery might solicit our freedom, then the vial would be handed over despite the lack of guarantees. Lipinski, however, did not appear to be the murderous type.

The sergeant returned and came straight to me. "Well, Mr. Conroy. Do you know where it is?"

I stood and eyed him through my visor. "I think I do—it appears I misunderstood the clue. The vial is not down here—it's up there." I pointed to the overhanging cliff wall.

He squinted through his visor at the cliff and commented, "Are you sure?"

"As sure as I'll ever be. If it's not there then I am at a loss."

"That's one hell of a fucking climb!"

"My father used his valet to hide the vial and then wiped the location's memory. Can you unscramble its processor?"

"You had better not be messing with my mind, Mr. Conroy. It will have serious consequences for you."

I repeated my request. "Just reverse the scrambling and I'll ask the android to retrieve the vial."

Lapinski opened an aluminum case which lay in the grass nearby and produced the electromagnetic disrupter.

Several minutes later, the android's processor came alive and the blue light of his eyes oscillated with rapid succession. A moment later Happydoo sat up to look around in surprise.

'I seemed to have had a break in my service. Is that you, Master Beckett?'

I welcomed him back to AI existence. "Happydoo, these men would like you to retrieve the vial for them."

'I see the grave has been almost completely dug up. There is no memory of finding it. Do you know where it is, Master Beckett? I would be happy to retrieve it for you.'

I pointed to a spot high above on the rock face of the cliff overhang. "It should be up there on one of those ledges. I read the clue incorrectly. Set yourself to rock-climbing mode and see if you can find it."

The android gave me the proverbial answer and headed off toward the cliff. Happydoo climbed the rock face with a confidence humans did not have. The built-in survey-scan apparatus, with nano-cameras situated in his eyes, provided a capability to break down the wall into quadrants and highlight every tiny crack or fissure within a hands grasp.

He reached the first ledge after ten minutes and scanned it for the vial. A few seconds later, a small metal box appeared in his grasp and the info-vial, at last, became a reality.

When Happydoo returned to the base of the cliff wall, he handed the small metal box to me. I offered it to Lapinski who took it without comment. "You have what you came for—now please let us go."

He opened the metal box and removed the vial to examine it more closely. "I am afraid we have plans for Miss Jenson—but you are free to go, Mr. Conroy."

My blood froze. "What plans are you talking about?"

"Mr. Jameson told us to bring her back to the WGF offices."

The emotion in my voice betrayed my love for Carla. "I won't leave her! You must take me back with you."

"It's out of the question, Mr. Conroy—I have my orders."

For the first time since the team arrested us, Carla spoke. "Leave it be, Beckett. I'll be fine."

I shot her a confused glance. "How do you know?"

"Because if they harm me, it will unleash a much greater problem for them."

"What is it you are not telling me, Carla?"

She looked away from my fierce glare and said nothing.

After a moment's silence, Lapinski resolved the mystery for me. "She works for the NWEIA."

I stared at Carla, the truth finally sinking in. "Why didn't you tell me?"

She moved closer to me and her eyes held my own with intensity. "I wanted to, but it didn't seem right at the time."

To put things together in difficult situations did not always come with any ease for me.

"So let me get this straight—you have been deceiving me these past few days—you wanted the info-vial as much as these blood-suckers and you were prepared to lead me on to get it."

Carla became a little indignant at my outburst. "I wasn't after the info-vial, Beckett, but the people behind the attempt to steal it."

Lapinski jumped in at this point. "We don't have time for this." With a motion to Tree-trunk and the third member of the team, he indicated their departure. Carla, with a laser gun stuck into her back followed on behind the sergeant, to the hidden transporter. I stood, deeply confused with emotions in turmoil, while the group moved along the riverbed. Twice, before they went beyond the embankment, Carla turned to look back at me.

Happydoo focused his visual senses on me. *'Are you okay, Master Beckett?'*

After a few moments my composure returned. "Let's get back to the hideaway. We need to return to Quantum City as quickly as possible."

A roar of antigravity propulsion emanated from beyond the embankment and a transporter with WGF insignia displayed on the side, lifted above the rocky outcrop and flew off in an easterly direction. My heart skipped a beat as I thought about what might happen to Carla—my only hope lay in her intuition with regard to Jameson not harming her. The more I thought about it the more the likelihood for I felt trepidation for Carla's hopes. Dr. Jameson might feel he no further options remained but to dispose of her.

We reached the hideaway as darkness fell, which brought with it a fabulous display of the Aurora. I wasted no time but went straight out to our antigrav. A perturbed Happydoo followed in my wake and kept up a commentary to let me know he would be happy to tidy things up if I could wait another ten minutes.

Within a short space of time we cleared the launch pad and the transporter's computer received its command to return us to the Quantum City spaceport.

∞∞

Twenty-Four

Deciding a Course of Action

Happydoo and I endured an uneventful trip back to the Orion Hotel. My thoughts, preoccupied with Carla's abduction by the WGF security team, ranged from fear to anger. The question, as to whether we would ever see one another again, still plagued me. Despite my anger over the omission in regard to her real professional identity, I still desired to be with her.

My other concern—Freda's abduction by Nassir and his crew of shitheads. With the evening already well spent, I decided Uncle Sid should be informed of the status quo.

The android in charge of room administration assured me my uncle had not left the hotel, so I decided to pay his room a quick visit. A knock on his door drew no response so we returned to our room. On arrival the android parked itself in the charge booth and l climbed into the ablution chamber. All the exercise and trauma of the day's events left me tired and ready for bed.

The light turned off at my command and I lay awake for a minute or two in reflection of Carla's fate, when the hotel com burst into life and Uncle Sid's voice shattered the silence of the room.

"Beckett? Are you there?"

"Yes, I'm here—almost asleep; I guess you want to talk?"

"If it's not too much trouble. I understand you're probably tired but I need to touch base with you."

"No Problem, Uncle Sid. I'll see you in the bar in about five."

Over the course of two whiskeys Uncle Sid heard the entire story of our visit to Eagle's Nest. He told his own story of the search for Freda and the dearth of information gathered from various contacts.

"I don't know what to do—I'm going out of my mind with worry."

He followed up with a suspicion of Carla's involvement and wondered if she might not have colluded with Jameson, to gain the info-vial.

My ilk rose a little at his words. "She's an NWEIA agent, Uncle Sid. How could she be involved? It seems more likely to me the EIA are on the trail of the info-vial for reasons of international security."

Uncle Sid remained unconvinced. "When you've lived as long as I have, you learn things."

I tried to avoid the escalation of inner emotion. Nothing would be gained by an argument and his words made some sense. A doubt, about Carla, impinged on my blind trust and I decided to change the subject.

"What are we going to do about the vial?"

Uncle Sid took a sip of his drink. "I'm not sure. With it being in WGF hands we're screwed as far as Freda is concerned. Maybe Nassir will know Jameson has the vial—they could be working together."

I added my perspective. "We have until the fourth—another three days before we are due to come up with the vial for Nassir—we still have time to find her."

He stifled a yawn. "Let's sleep on it tonight. It's getting late and I'm worn out."

I drained the last drops of my whiskey, and together we left the lounge for our rooms.

Sleep came with some difficulty. Despite the physical drain over the past few days my mind still wanted to work overtime. Carla's beautiful face played a huge role in my thoughts, but it all came to rest and my consciousness drifted into dreamland.

*

In the morning, at the breakfast table, the subject resumed with the previous evening's intensity. I felt our most valuable asset in Freda's case rested with the time that remained before Nassir required the vial. The most logical plan would be to inform the police of her disappearance.

With Carla, on the other hand, my patience showed no such restraint. This came, not because I thought any less of Freda, but more from the need to resolve Carla's position in this whole debacle. My most urgent need lay at the feet of Confucius—a social justice and sincerity concern—on whose side of the equation did she feature?

I needed to know before my feelings for her passed the point of no return. A huge disappointment lay in the offing if Uncle Sid's accusations found any credibility. On the other hand, if my gut-feel turned out to be correct, there might be a future for my new-found infatuation.

"I am going to make contact with the EIA and tell them what's happened. If Jameson is holding Carla they would have the resources to free her."

Uncle Sid looked doubtful. "I don't know if it's a wise thing to do, Beckett. They may suspect you of being involved in her disappearance. Worst still, if something bad happens to her—they may accuse you of orchestrating the whole thing."

"I'll have to take that risk. I can't sit here not knowing what's going on. Maybe they will help us find Freda."

Uncle Sid nodded. "Yes, it's possible. However, I 'm concerned, at this point in time, about anyone in an official capacity knowing about Freda's disappearance. There's no telling what Nassir might do to her if he finds out we've gone to the authorities."

I thought about his point of view. "You may be right—I won't say anything about Freda but Carla is one of their operatives, and they deserve to know what's happened to her."

"Suit yourself, Beckett, but I advise against it."

We left it at that. After breakfast I went back to my room to find the local address for the New World Earth Intelligence Agency. Happydoo, all charged up greeted me with his typical, *'I'm happy to see you, Master Beckett,'* and some of the tension of the morning's conversation with my uncle, drained away.

The omninet would provide the location I needed.

"We are going to pay the EIA a visit, Happydoo. I need to tell them about Miss Jenson."

The android did a little jig and twisted its synthetic, facial skin to form a grin. I wondered if it really understood the possible ramifications of our intended mission. Happydoo may yet surprise me—the android's latest upgrade showed great promise.

Armed with the EIA's physical address, we left the Orion and headed toward the building where Central housed its continental connection for Quantum City. The adjoined EIA department took up a full block and stood fourteen stories high. Two military androids stood at attention, dressed in the EIA's standard issue, one on each side of the entrance. The programming of Military androids and bots made them the only AI to be licensed with a potential to harm humankind.

The Military and Intelligence Agencies combined into one service at the end of the Great War, enjoyed a worldwide oversight. The integration of the two services came about when a lack of human leadership, brought on by the continued decrease in population, became a factor.

The intension to phase out all human troops in favor of bots and androids became a priority with the formation of battle-droid battalions. Human operatives, however, still enjoyed the bulk of intelligence gathering, mainly to observe the fanatical religious element, largely the cause of the Great War. The fall off of terrorism changed the military's mandate, which now focused more on monitoring of potential uprisings, against The Administration. The EIA involved its operatives with the follow-up on industrial espionage and high profile embezzlement of credits. Cases, such as my dad's intellectual property wrangle, would be high on their list. The gift of longevity for the human race could not be allowed to fall into the wrong hands.

∞∞

Twenty-Five

Special Agent Sylvia Duke

The android receptionist greeted us with polite professionalism and asked what the nature of our business entailed. Not sure who to ask for, I settled for a not-to-specific answer to its question.

"We would like to speak to the special agent in charge of local, non-religious intelligence gathering."

The android cocked its head to one side in typical fashion.

'And what would be the subject of your en-quiries?'

I took a stab in the dark. "It's to do with the A-Mortal Gene brief."

The receptionist immediately buzzed a few electronic signals into what must have been someone's CCT and said, *'Please wait for Special Agent Duke. She will be down shortly to speak to you.'*

Relieved to have struck a chord, Happydoo and I waited for agent Duke to arrive. Our surroundings, presented the atmosphere of a modern museum. Tubular showcases, which contained uniformed androids with weapons in hand and encapsulated for posterity, took up the center of the foyer.

The floor tiles, a special lightweight, graphene glass, lit from an innate power source caused the entire floor to glow incandescently—the walls appeared to be constructed of a shiny marble stone. Holographic portraits of humans, I assumed to be operative managers or directors of the EIA, resided within apse-like niches along the extended hallway. The entire visage gave the impression of high efficiency, supported by the latest technology—a formidable bastion of arcane intelligence-gathering and industriousness, backed by exceptional military might.

While we stood in awe of our surroundings, I didn't envy Carla in a place like this. Agent Duke, a slim, tough looking woman with graying hair, interrupted my thoughts. She greeted us with a nod, and stuck out her hand to grasp mine with a strong grip.

"Special Agent, Sylvia Duke. How can I help you?"

I introduced myself and Happydoo, who remained in the background. I noticed Duke exuded a business-like attitude with her rigid stance and stony features. My guess at the cause of her apparent attitude—she did not expect anyone outside the correct jurisdiction, to know about the A-Mortal Gene brief.

At the mention of my name she visibly relaxed a little; perhaps in the realization that the son of the man responsible for one of life's most recent and foremost discoveries, should rate somewhere amongst the knowledgeable of the brief's existence.

My answer to her question reflected the need to come straight to the point.

"Agent, Carla Jenson, contacted me a few days ago to tell me she could help in my quest to find the info-vial, which contains the latest details of my father's genetic breakthrough."

Duke stiffened in response to my news.

"And what about her?"

"We were out at my dad's hideaway home in the Eagle Mountains when a security team from the WGF arrived to take us prisoner. I had to give them the vial. They took Miss Jenson prisoner, but allowed the android and myself to go free. I'm concerned for her safety."

The agent in charge nodded. "The WGF contacted us a while back to ask for our assistance in tracking down the vial. Dr. Jameson said the discovery rated as their intellectual property and could be in danger of being abused if it fell into the wrong hands."

My response included the usual impetuousness with which I approached ironical matters.

"It's Jameson and his crowd who want to exploit the discovery, which by the way, belongs to my father and not to the WGF."

Duke looked amused.

"Who actually owns the discovery is not for me to decide. Agent Jenson was placed in situ to keep an eye on who might be threatening your father. As far as we are concerned, the discovery becomes the WGF's property in lieu of it being worked on by a member of their staff."

I could see her point but the anger in me still simmered at Carla's incarceration by Jameson.

"The WGF directors all stand to gain from this discovery, and I believe Carla Jenson found out exactly what they were up to. Have you spoken to her recently?"

Sylvia Duke folded her arms. "Yes, in fact we have—Miss Jensen did not mention anything regarding wrong doing by the WGF."

Incredulous at her statement, the question shot from my lips, "You've spoken to her since her return from Eagle's Nest?"

"Yes, I have. Don't be tempted to think we know nothing about what's going on here. I have placed her on stress leave for the time being, until she gets her head sorted out."

"Stress leave—what does that mean?"

"It means, Mr. Conroy, you don't get to talk to her. My suggestion is you leave things as they are and allow us to do our job."

My anger brimmed over. "Tell me where she's gone. I need to see her."

Duke smirked. "I cannot do that."

I came close to punching the bitch but some good sense prevailed. I turned on my heel and grunted. "Let's get the fuck out of here—we're wasting valuable time."

My thunderous stare received a resolute glower from the agent in charge as I looked back over my shoulder at her.

Happydoo made a laconic comment. *'That went well, didn't it, Master Beckett?'*

My present mood prevented a civil answer and we jumped onto the escalator. I hoped a return visit to the NWEIA would never become a future necessity.

∞∞

Twenty-Six

The Enemy of my Enemy is my Friend

At the hotel, a surprise awaited me in the form of a message. I recognized the voice to be Dr. Jameson's, with a request to meet with me. My words to Happydoo with regard to Jameson were not very complimentary. At first, I wanted to decline but Uncle Sid, whom we met for lunch in the lounge, felt it would be wise to find out what the old man was up to.

"It's better to know what your enemy is planning," he said.

I called Jameson on the omninet. His response came back within a minute.

"Dr. Sutton will be there in ten minutes. I know you are probably pissed off at the moment, but I think you should hear him out—I would come myself but the old legs are not what they used to be."

"You expect me to cooperate after sending in your pit bulls to terrorize us, Dr. Jameson? You already have the vial! What are you after this time—my autograph?"

"All I ask for is you listen to what Dr. Sutton has to say—then you can decide the future."

I finally agreed to the request, only because of intrigue. The WGF already had the vial—what could they possibly want from me?"

At 1400 hours, Dr. Sutton entered the bar lounge and made his way to our table. Happydoo had gone off to central's warehouse for a processor tweak. Dr. Sutton stopped at the chair opposite mine and looked solemnly at the two of us.

"I am here to share something of impor-tance with you, may I sit?"

Uncle Sid nodded and Sutton sat adjacent to me. His obese figure covered the chair like a de-flating balloon. The man's jowls flapped slightly when he spoke and the weak chin seemed destined to disappear at times.

"I know what you must be thinking—our interruption of your stay in the Eagle Mountains must appear like a strong-armed invasion and the vial, being our intellectual property, is question-able to you."

He stopped to wipe away the accumulated perspiration from his brow and continued.

"Dr. Jameson is, however, willing to negoti-ate a fair settlement with you over the matter of ownership—."

Sutton gazed at me with brown, pig-like eyes and mopped his brow again.

"—Dr. Jameson's sentiments, regarding the treatment you received are sympathetic. He calls it an 'unfortunate situation.'

I looked Sutton in the eyes and said, "But you have the vial—why the sudden sentiment? Surely you don't really care what my uncle and I feel about it? You have what you wanted."

Sutton gave a weak smile. "The information is incomplete. The details of research in the vial are exactly the same given you by Miss Jenson, prior to your leaving for Eagle's Nest."

His words momentarily stunned me and I felt at a loss for words. Uncle Sid jumped into the conversation

"You're saying there is no indication of the breakthrough—the latter part of the research is missing?"

"Correct. Either Padraig Conroy is playing a game with us, or you've misread the clue he left you."

In my mind there appeared to be no way my dad would be playing a game with all of us. To what end, and to whose benefit? I still had questions for Dr. Sutton.

"I want to know what role Dr. Nassir is playing in all of this?"

Sutton looked a little sheepish. "Dr. Nassir does what he does—he is only trying, on behalf of the WGF, to get the vial and I can't speak for him."

Uncle Sid thumped the table. "He went too far when he abducted my personal assistant as collateral for Beckett turning over the vial."

Sutton's shock may have been faked but I couldn't be sure.

"I don't know anything about abduction but I will speak to Dr. Jameson. If Dr. Nassir is operating outside the WGF security code he will be disciplined, I can assure you of that."

Uncle Sid gave Sutton a threatening stare and wagged his finger.

"You tell Jameson from me—if one hair on Miss Banning's head is harmed we will be coming after both of you."

Dr. Sutton remained calm. "There is no need to make threats, Mr. Conroy. I'll speak to Dr. Jameson about this. It's not the way we operate, and if we find Dr. Nassir guilty of this accusation, we will take it further."

I still needed to know where Carla fitted into the story.

"Tell me about Miss Jenson. What's her involvement with the WGF's quest to get the vial?"

Sutton pursed his lips and thought for a moment.

"Miss Jenson was brought in at Dr. Jameson's request. We suspected someone threatened your father and wanted to acquire access to his work. As an EIA operative she assumed a position within our company with the hope of flushing out the instigator."

Sutton's information appeared to confirm Sylvia Duke's record.

"So, when Sergeant Lapinski brought Carla back with him, you released her from her duties?"

"Special Agent Duke told us about your visit. Yes, we released Miss Jenson because she had blown her cover."

I still wondered what Carla would have done if the WGF had not relieved us of the vial. Would she have allowed me to keep what I believed to be my inherited property, or would she have taken it from me at gun-point? I pondered on the thought of seeing her again, with the idea of resolving the matter.

Dr. Sutton pushed on. "We both sit with a problem. Neither of us has the information we are looking for.

I felt a measure of agitation. "So, you want me to see if there isn't something I have missed in reading the clue?"

"Correct. There could be another vial in a different place. I knew your father reasonably well. He sometimes bordered on paranoia, and being such a shrewd person it's possible he felt extra precautions were needed."

In consideration of Sutton's argument, the proposition seemed possible.

"And if I find the real information, what is Dr. Jameson proposing?"

"We will draw up a contract to share any proceeds of the outcome. Dr. Jameson believes the WGF as provider of the opportunity, should have the benefit and your father be accredited with the discovery. This is the way these things generally work. A bonus will be awarded for the work done, which would be passed on to you. "

I couldn't argue with his position apart from saying, "My father obviously did not see it that way. If I agree to your proposal I would be going against his wishes."

"I understand your sentiments on the matter but you must make a decision. I believe the proposition to be more than fair," retorted Sutton.

Uncle Sid and I looked at each other not knowing how to respond in the moment. Finally, I decided to play it safe.

"If you and Dr. Jameson can try to determine what has happened to Miss Banning and obtain her release, then I will consider the proposition."

"I will let Dr. Jameson know your concerns regarding Miss Banning. Once we have spoken to Dr. Nassir to corroborate the information you have given us, I will contact you. If he has violated the WGF code of conduct we will discipline him most severely."

I nodded my agreement and the meeting came to a conclusion. Some investigation regarding the clue my father had left lay ahead and I needed time to think.

∞∞

Twenty-Seven

A Meeting with the Directors

After Dr. Sutton heaved his fat-ass out of the hotel, Uncle Sid and I sat drank our whiskeys and reviewed the encounter. Half an hour later, with the post mortem over, I ordered another bottle and retired to my room. It would be a good time for me to deliberate on two issues: Carla and the research information.

By 2200 hours, my condition could only be described as a state of considerable inebriation. Happydoo became alarmed by my conduct and the remarks, which no longer made any sense to him. Eventually he retired to the charge booth, in fear I would throw something at him.

With my mental stability overwhelmed, sleep came at the price of several nightmares. Visions of Eagle's Nest, where my father's eyes stared aloofly at me plus a romp in bed with Freda, sanctioned by an angry Carla, vied for the most vivid of dreams. The morning came as a final blessing, to end the night's long perambulations in a sinister world of silent torture.

Accompanied by a headache, my mouth tasted like the bottom of a parrot's cage. The resurrection, urged on by the rays of sunlight, which illuminated the almost-empty bottle of Supernova on a side-table, reminded me why I felt so bad. After a quick cleanup and ablution I set the in-house, refreshment replicator to provide a mug of cafteen, while my mind surfaced from its half-dead state.

Happydoo peeped out from the booth to see if the ambiance was safe enough for an appearance. His greeting brought a half-smile to my lips.

'*I'm happy to see you have survived the night, Master Beckett.*'

"My apologies, Happydoo. I trust you weren't indisposed in any way by my enthusiasm?"

The android raised a knuckle to its synthetic mouth in predictable fashion and chuckled with the inclusion of a bob-and-weave action.

'*Good one, Master Beckett, good one.*'

"I've been thinking about our next course of action, Happydoo. Do you have any suggestions?"

'I have been reviewing our options in the light of the situation. In my opinion, it seems logical for us to seek Dr. Jameson's help, Master Beckett.'

You could have knocked me over with tissue paper. This so-called machine had actually reviewed our situation and come up with a plan.

"How do you figure that, Happydoo?"

Delighted, the android performed the pirouette and foot-stamp routine. *'The WGF are after the research for reasons of promoting genetic endeavor. If they believe Dr. Nassir is trying to use it for his own profit they will surely help us find Miss Freda. If we can find Dr. Nassir, we will find her too. We need to gain their cooperation, Master Beckett.'*

"I'm, not so sure the discovery of the A-Mortal Gene really belongs to them. It was my dad's wish I gain the full control of it."

'That is true, Master Beckett, but we may have a greater chance of finding Miss Freda if we can locate Dr. Nassir. You still hold a trump

card—no one knows where the research is. You have some time to work this out. If push comes to shove, you can always make the deal Dr. Jameson is offering.'

The android's idea made sense. I needed a greater resource to help flush Nassir out and obtain Freda's release. The WGF could provide it with their security division. Despite having held me up at gunpoint Lapinski had not seemed such a bad guy.

"I guess that's true, Happydoo. I need to revisit the clue and see what it is I'm missing. But finding Miss Freda is a priority."

I dropped a CCT, along with other items into my leg-pocket, and then caught the verticap down to the dining room for breakfast. The morning meal, due to an absence of patrons, ensued in relative silence. With breakfast over, I asked the android to connect with the WGF office via its omninet communicator and we waited for Dr. Sutton to come online. A short while later Fat-Ass's voice boomed from the android's mouthpiece.

"Dr. Sutton, here."

"Dr. Sutton? It's Beckett Conroy. I need to talk with Dr. Jameson."

Several minutes later we left the Orion to make our way to the WGF offices. A meeting with Doctors' Jameson and Sutton had been arranged; they waited for me to update them on the latest news with regard to the research material's location. I stopped short, however, of any promised agreement to Jameson's conditions of a deal—the priority, for me remained the safe return of Freda.

A middle-aged woman met us at the verti-cap exit on the building's top floor. Memories of Carla flooded back to bring a renewed sense of longing, as Happydoo and I followed the woman along the hallway, to Dr. Jameson's office.

The two doctors greeted us with enthusiasm. Initiated by quick handshakes, we got down to business and the conversation began in earnest. The sense of a common goal permeated the atmosphere and for the first time, both parties appeared to be on the same side. The element of trust, however, still remained a barrier for me—the WGF's conviction lacked substance and sincerity. I got the impression of the director's collusion toward personal gain. The goal, to work for humankind's common good seemed to have lost ground in favor of the foundation and its member's personal profit.

Dr. Jameson regaled the virtues of my father's efforts and emphasized the importance of mutual cooperation. His pontification continued for some time with the occasional interruption from Dr. Sutton.

"This is a great opportunity for the WGF to make an un-rivaled contribution to the progress of modern genetics. It will secure a great amount of prestige and support for the work we are doing."

I listened with patience and acknowledged their drivel with the occasional nod of the head.

"So you see, Beckett—we only want what is good for posterity. Humankind is on the decline and if it continues at its present rate we will become extinct as a species by the year 2500 C.E."

It all sounded logical, but behind Jameson's coal-black eyes, I sensed something else: a sinister, cold, and calculated purpose. It caused a shudder to run down my spine.

Dr. Sutton's jowls flapped with vigor while he, in turn, re-enforced Jameson's point of view.

"Your father, Beckett, has obviously discovered a way to retain the integrity of a human cell's telomeres. As you would know, the telomere is the weak link of all DNA strands, being the caps that protect the chromosomes. I'm looking forward to seeing his final research."

Throughout this flood of nonsense, my reactions remained cordial. Happydoo sat like a statue, without comment, and listened to the conversation. When they both ran out of justifications and scientific perambulations, I brought the meeting back to the mutual point of concern. "What about Dr. Nassir? He is holding Miss Banning in some location my uncle and I have not been able to find as yet. According to his instructions to me I need to turn over the research material by July fourth before he will release her."

Jameson looked thoughtful. "Dr. Nassir put in for two weeks leave and hasn't been in the office over the past few days. Our security division is busy trying to establish his whereabouts."

My annoyance erupted. "I am not prepared to share the location of the research if Miss Banning is not found and released. If you'll help us get her back, I'll talk about turning over the vial—when I find it."

Sutton shifted his fat-ass to a more comfortable position.

"We only have your word for this—I'm sure we will be able to come to a logical conclusion for Dr. Nassir's actions once we locate him. We will trust you on turning over the research."

My tirade was not yet over. "There is also the question of your secretary, Miss Jenson."

Jameson's eyes seemed to morph into two deep-space objects.

"Ah, yes. Miss Jenson—our favorite little EIA agent. She appears to have acted beyond her mandate. Miss Duke, of the NWEIA, has replaced her with another girl."

"Do you know where Miss Jenson can be contacted," I asked.

Sutton jumped in. "I'm afraid we have no address for her. You'll have to ask the EIA."

Having drawn a blank on Carla my hopes for our reconciliation seemed even more remote now.

"What are you going to do about Miss Banning?"

Jameson rubbed his chin with thumb and forefinger.

"I would suggest you just sit tight and wait for our sergeant Lapinski to come up with something on Dr. Nassir. When we have discussed the matter with Nassir we will contact you."

I thought about his answer and it appeared I would not be allowed me to be a part of the investigation.

"I want to go with your Mr. Lapinski. My android and I could be of help. If you disagree I will feel obliged to go to the police."

Dr. Jameson considered my request for a moment.

"We feel it would be counter-productive and premature to bring the police in on this. Once we have established Dr. Nassir's reasons for his actions we might consider that avenue. I will tell

Lapinski to accommodate you and your android, but you do so at your own risk."

"Agreed," I retorted.

Dr. Jameson stood and came around the large desk to grab my hand in his scrawny paw. "I'm sure we'll get the bottom of this whole thing."

∞∞

Twenty-Eight

Joining Forces with the WGF

We left Jameson's office, with directions to Sergeant Lapinski's lair in the basement of the building. The verticap deposited us in the cold security foyer, where Lapinski waited. He guided us down another long hallway to his office.

The rough concrete basement, void of windows, décor and paint, presented a distinct military bunker atmosphere; our footsteps echoed off the walls and ceiling—it sounded like the inside of a large steel pipe.

Lapinski's office turned out to be a stark cubicle with a small, metal desk in one corner. The single ceiling light provided a dull luminescence and cast eerie shadows against the four barren walls.

The chairs lacked design and provided little in the way of comfort. Lapinski exuded the impression of the quintessential combatant—tough and hard as nails.

"So, you want to be in on the mission? What, if I may ask, is your prime motivation?"

"My reason for tagging along is to make sure Miss Banning has not been harmed and Dr. Nassir gets what is coming to him."

Lapinski sounded almost sympathetic. "I will do what I can but finding the research information is the prime goal."

"Then we understand each other. Happydoo and I will do our best not to get in your way. Do you have any leads?"

Lapinski turned on the holographic viewer embedded in the desktop and brought up a hologram of the city's layout.

"The EIA are conducting their own investigation, so we have to be careful to stay out of each other's hair. My research on Nassir's assets shows a warehouse on the corner of Bohr and Lorentz streets, plus an apartment in Einstein Ridge."

"The warehouse is more than familiar to me," I said. "But, it would be too conspicuous a place to keep hostages."

Lapinski ran a sinewy hand through his military-style haircut.

"I'm looking for a place where he could carry out experiments—he wouldn't need much space and I suspect the apartment might be a possibility. It too, is a bit conspicuous, though."

"Why don't we start with the warehouse and the apartment first."

"I intend to do precisely that," the sergeant answered. "We need to get moving."

The WGF security antigrav hovered ten centimeters above the ground while we all clambered in. Lapinski, Tree-trunk and the third member of the team, a man called Dickson plus Happydoo and myself, all crushed into the confined passenger space. Lapinski called the computer coordinates and the transporter took off. The vehicle, one of the few licensed transporters allowed on the streets of Quantum City, which flew along at a height of five meters, whisked between the buildings and skipped over intersections.

A few minutes later we pulled up on the corner of Bohr and Lorentz. The warehouse brought back bad memories of the Ugly one and caused me to experience a moment's paralysis, which prevented my immediate exit from the anti-grav. The inertia lasted for a brief moment before I overcame it and stumbled onto the sidewalk.

The entrance to the building had seen better days. The double doors appeared to be unlocked and the absence of a cleanup service became evident by the mess of empty fast-food cartons outside the entrance. Our party entered with a militia-styled stealth and looked around the inner area for anything suspicious. Tree-trunk held his laser rifle at the ready, while Lapinski and Dickson sported hand lasers. Happydoo and I carried no arms.

Upstairs, the main room provided us with no evidence to base any assumptions on. The chair and the straps still lay on the floor where I last saw them. The scene remained as I remembered it and a shudder coursed through my body at the thought of the shitheads and their callousness.

"There's nothing here," said Lapinski. "Anything you can add, Mr. Conroy?"

I shook my head. "No, let's get out of here. This place gives me the fucking creeps."

We moved out of the main room and trooped down the stairs to the entrance.

"That leaves the apartment," I said.

Everyone clambered back into the antigrav and we took off.

The buildings at Einstein Ridge, the most modern constructs of Quantum City's real estate industry, exhibited long rows of apartments. The complexes contained a multitude of one-bedroom abodes and ranged upward, to whole-floor, single dwellings, which all basked in the sunlight under the city's graphene-glass dome.

Dr. Nassir's apartment turned out to be a penthouse and took up the entire floor of a building. This arrangement supported owners who earned credits above a level one. A verticap took us to the top floor where we poured onto the landing and approached the apartment's front entrance. Several attempts to locate the control pad for the door's opaque colored force-field came up unsuccessful, until Happydoo told Lapinski to look in the top lintel region of the entrance. The sergeant thrust his gloved hand into the overhead lintel's center and the pad appeared.

Tree-trunk peered at the control. "It's one of the latest type locks. I'm not sure we will be able to find the code."

Happydoo came to the rescue again. *'Sir, I would be happy to help. Allow me to access the pad. I possess a unique feature, a mini quantum code detection processor. It is courtesy of central's latest android upgrading.'*

Tree-trunk scowled at the android but stepped back. Happydoo placed the back of his hand on the pad. His eyes glowed and emitted a narrow blue beam, aimed at a tiny receiver in the hand's palm. After ten seconds the force field retracted and we stepped inside.

Lapinski nodded at Happydoo in approval and then looked at me.

"It's a good thing we brought the android."

Happydoo's classical pirouette followed, accompanied by one of his programmed range of chuckles.

"He keeps surprising me," I said.

The apartment furnishings exuded luxury— Dr. Nassir lived extremely well, perhaps too well for a level one earner. Another level of earnings, enjoyed by a few, existed beyond the sort-after level one—Level 0. This level entertained those privileged to run lucrative businesses. My thoughts began to race—it appeared Dr. Nassir lived a lifestyle of someone who enjoyed the proceeds of such a credit level.

The apartment appeared to be void of people. An extensive search of all the rooms produced nothing. It did not even appear to have been lived in for a while.

We made ready to leave, disappointed at the lack of evidence that might lead us to Nassir's present hideout. Then Happydoo called me from one of the three ablution quarters.

'Master Beckett! Would you please come and look at this.'

Lapinski and I rushed to the quarters to see what held the android's interest.

Happydoo pointed to the shelf of a wall closet and we looked hard to identify what he indicated—a vial of pills. None of us would have picked this up. Six tablet pill-vials took up most of the shelf and all appeared to have Dr. Nassir's name on the labels—all except one.

I lifted it from amongst the others and to my astonishment saw the name: F. Banning. Bingo—Freda's medication. The vial's contents indicated a type of mood-swing prevention medication.

Freda carried these drugs on her at all times. She must have been desperate to leave a clue of some sort and the vial confirmed her presence in the apartment. Thank the stars for Happydoo—we would have missed the clue altogether but not for him.

The contents of the vial revealed one item and it wasn't a pill.

"It's a small round emblem. I haven't seen this insignia before—it looks like a small badge of some sort and appears to have a magnetic base."

Happydoo craned forward to peer at the item.

'I would be happy to submit an image of this to the omninet-pedia section, Master Beckett. There has to be media use of it somewhere in the world.'

"Great idea, Happydoo. Freda must have found it here in the apartment and decided to leave it as a clue."

Lapinski nodded his approval and the android went to work again. Its presence made our task much easier—it took less than a minute for the omni-pedia to produce the answer to our quest.

Happydoo related the product description. *'The emblem represents a product brand-name called* Hyper Performance, *an anabolic hormone performance enhancer for athletes. The drug is sold in every pharmaceutical outlet on the continent and beyond.'*

Lapinski scratched his ear. "What does it mean?"

Stumped for an answer I went further into Happydoo's transmission of the pedia site.

"The drug is produced by only one company per regional sector, of which there are twelve sectors covering the New World Earth's total pharmaceutical distribution outlets. The production of anabolic hormone enhancer for sector-one is situated here, in Quantum City."

It did not take long to locate the factory's name and address—the Hercules Manufacturing Company.

I felt a sense of excitement. "The HMC's premises are on the outskirts of the city, a section zoned for light industry. The address is forty-seven Southern Cross Street, Constellation Park."

Lapinski made a motion for us to move out. "Let's see if the address delivers anything interesting."

I silently thanked Freda for her foresight. The clue made sense. Nassir gave the impression of high roller status—someone who lived well above his means. If his extra income came from business, the HMC must be the reason. His work at the WGF would also place him in a position to pursue the latest innovations in drugs. It all began to make perfect sense.

The WGF transporter flew with silent authority along the streets. Only Vehicles licensed for intercity travel could use the city's main commercial area—mostly official first responders or police units. The owners of private transport parked their units in special warehouse facilities, at various accessible points, on the city's outer limits. Any un-licensed transport, within the prohibited zone would be shut down by Central, the master control computer.

Twenty minutes later we reached the city outskirts. The onboard computer guided the transporter into a lane, which ran adjacent to a large industrial building. The late afternoon sun-light radiated through the dome above, but pro-vided little warmth to the air. The transporter parked and we, with a minimum of fuss, all scram-bled out onto the pavement.

Our group made its way quietly along the wall toward the rear of the building. The adren-aline rush caught me in the moment, to bring with it a moment of queasiness but I pushed through and kept my focus on the task at hand. With lasers at the ready, we converged on the back entrance, the one visible ingress to the building.

Without a prompt from me, Happydoo went to work on the force-field code. A movement-sen-sitive light came on to scare the shit out of us as we huddled around the android but it continued with the process, until the force field retracted.

With this barrier out of the way we moved along a back corridor to check each room, which for the most, contained cartons and factory products. Occasional pieces of outdated, derelict machinery and spare parts, dotted the floor. One wall sported a presentation of the emblem discovered in Nassir's apartment—the clue.

The corridor ended at a stairway that led to the second level of the three-story building. Lapinski took the lead, followed by Tree-trunk and then Dickson, all with their weapons at the ready.

Happydoo and I brought up the rear. The security team would be the first in the line of fire, if things went south. It did not take long for our clandestine entrance to draw attention.

∞∞

Twenty-Nine

Nassir's Factory

A red strobe light at the top of the stairway began its oscillations, accompanied by an alarm, to announce the discovery of our break-in. I wanted to run back along the corridor to stairs but a force field snapped into place behind us, and prevented any escape. One direction remained—forward.

Lapinski turned and motioned us to keep up.

"Stay together."

Happydoo and I obeyed as we hunched over and broke into a jog. The alarm grew louder with an increase in intensity but still we saw no one. The upper corridor opened into a large room filled with manufacturing equipment. At the end of the room, a control panel lined the one wall with platforms that showed holograms of different parts of the process. A digitized voice floated across the open space:

SECURITY BREACH, BACK CORRIDOR,
SECURITY BREACH, BACK CORRIDOR....

A laser beam shot out from somewhere in front of us, to burn a huge hole in the wall above Lapinski's head. We all hit the deck and made a vain attempt to see where the fire came from, but the sheer volume of equipment obstructed our view.

"Keep your heads down," shouted Lapinski.

Tree-trunk crawled like a leopard and managed to maneuver his body into a position for a better view of the holographic control visuals. He fired off a blast of super-heated light that appeared to do little damage before a retaliatory beam, shot out and hit him on the upper torso. A plume of sparks and smoke obscured our view and when I looked again, Tree-trunk lay spread-eagled, his body motionless. The laser lay on the floor out of reach.

Never involved in a combat situation before and scared shitless, my body would not respond to my brain. There remained little anyone could do to help Tree-trunk. He appeared to be dead.

Lapinski called out to him but received no answer. Another laser beam shot from a different area, hit the sergeant in the face and the laser fell from his grasp, onto the floor.

The acrid smell of body flesh combined with smoke, permeated the room. I glanced upward to see where the fire came from and my eye caught a movement, high up on the wall. In one corner of the room, a wall-mounted laser became visible through the smoke. Whoever controlled the weapon operated it by remote from a concealed area. This explained the lack of any visual on our assailants.

Dickson looked mortified. The entire mission faced a disaster. I lay flat on my stomach and with a quick backward glance made an attempt to establish the whereabouts of the android.

"Happydoo, where in shit's name are you?"

No answer. I pointed out the position of the wall-mounted laser to Dickson and he nodded. From his hiding place, behind the base of a cylindrical drum, he raised his laser to fire at the wall-mounted weapon. This time a beam came from a different direction to catch the unfortunate security officer on the side of the head. Smoke puffed out from his skull.   A multitude of electron-volts burned a hole through Dickson's cranium and he fell to the floor, like a sack of heavy soil.

Surrender appeared to be my only way out. With no guarantee of benevolence at the hands of my enemy, I stood with hands held high above my head.

"Don't shoot."

The laser on the wall swiveled toward me and for the first time in my life death beckoned. Perspiration burst out on my forehead as I looked around for the position of the camera, by which the weapon's operator could see the room. I found it near the ceiling. My ordeal to discover my fate would be revealed within the seconds that followed. I waited in the hope we had fallen to a a live human being and not a sophisticated, automated security system.

A familiar voice bellowed over an intercom.

"Welcome to our world, Conroy."

Oh no, dear God—the voice belonged to Pin-stripe.

"So, you found the little clue we left you," he said.

It now became clear that the clue left by Freda was orchestrated by the shitheads—a deliberate act of deception. Their aim, to get us onto their turf and eliminate us turned out to be horrific, but successful. It left me fearful of Freda's status and in doubt of my continued existence.

The moment of intense fear passed, replaced by anger—perhaps more at myself than my adversaries.

"What are you going to do with me?"

"Dr. Nassir would like a word with you before he disposes of the woman."

Pin-stripe's words brought little in the way of comfort to my ears. The question uppermost in my mind—could Happydoo still help me?

Did the shitheads know of the android's presence or had it somehow managed to escape their notice?

"Where is Miss Banning?" I asked.

"You'll be reunited with your old flame soon enough. Walk over to the exit in the back corner of the factory and come in. Don't try anything stupid."

With hands resting on my head, I did as directed. The entrance force-field retracted on approach and allowed me to exit the room of death. Beyond, a smaller room presented itself, with Pinstripe seated at a weapon's control system. He held a hand laser pointed at my chest and behind him stood my nemesis—Ugly-one. A huge smirk expressed the pure joy of once again, having me at his mercy.

"We meet again, Conroy. I am really beginning to enjoy our little confrontations."

I shuddered. "The only confrontation I want with you is to have you at my mercy—all I need is ten seconds."

Ugly-one almost doubled over with laughter.

"Listen to yourself. You're about as far from having me at your mercy as we are from fucking Pluto."

He approached with a look of menace. His fist shot out to catch me on the jaw—a light exploded in my brain, the floor came up to meet my unprotected face and I embarked on a journey down the long, dark tunnel to oblivion.

∞∞

Thirty

Imprisoned

I stirred from a vivid dream in which life took on the feel of fantasy. Someone's arms held me and I envisaged Carla's lovely face, close enough for her lips to gently caress mine, in sensual provocation.

The lips, however, did not belong to Carla. As I managed to crank one eyelid open, a woman's face with tear-streaked cheeks, accompanied by swollen, red eyes came into focus. I lurched sideways and rolled out of her grasp, confused by the sight my eyes beheld.

She gazed at me and reached out a hand of reassurance.

"Beck...please don't be frightened...it's me, Freda."

I raised the upper-half of my body, off the floor on weak, unsteady elbows, as recall went into action. Ugly-one must have unloaded a sucker-punch to my jaw with enough force to stop a buffalo in its tracks.

As the truth dawned on me our position took on a greater precariousness. Imprisoned by an evil, malevolent despot who would press me for information and then dispose of us, created the new reality.

"I'm sorry, Freda. My mind is just coming back online and I didn't mean to treat you with any disrespect."

I rose on painful knees to crawl back to her with my self-image at an all-time low.

"Please, forgive me."

My arms folded around her and she collapsed into my embrace, her body racked with desolate sobs. The trauma of the past few days of incarceration brought out all her pent up grief and she gave vent to it on my chest.

When the sobs reduced to occasional snorts, I asked a question.

"Do you still have those pills you take for your—"

She lowered her eyes. "I have enough for another day. One of those gangsters made me hand over the tablet-vial because they wanted to lure you here and make you think I left a clue."

"It worked pretty well," I said.

"I am so sorry, Beck. I never meant—"

"No, Freda—don't blame yourself. There was nothing you could have done differently. I'm just surprised he let you keep the pills."

"I guess he didn't want to deal with a crazy woman," she said. "I do sometimes forget to take them and the results are not good."

I dropped the subject and for the first time looked around in earnest at our surroundings.

The room lacked a window and sported one entrance, closed off by a force field. The ceiling, too high for me to reach, showed no sign of any trapdoors or visible weaknesses. In one corner an ablution module, roughly attached to the wall, appeared to have been a recent innovation.

An empty plate and mug sat on the floor, adjacent to the entrance. Their presence revealed a salient possibility—Nassir did not intend for us to starve—maybe he still planned to let us go after I produced the research. This dynamic might have changed, however, with our discovery of his lair.

A search of the entrance area revealed the force-field control, high on the top lintel of the door. It required a five digit code and after many wasted attempts at letters and number combinations, I gave up.

"I tried to find the right combo a number of times since I've been here," said Freda. "There's no way out."

"So I see—there remains one possibility, though."

She looked at me with trust in her eyes.

"Happydoo is somewhere in the building. I need to work out a way of contacting him."

Even as I said the words, a thought of possible salvation came to mind—the CCT which I took from my bedside that morning should still be in my pocket. I felt a measure of excitement.

"Maybe the two shitheads were negligent in checking me over."

A quick search of the pocket came up with nothing and a flush of disappointment flooded my soul. I tried the opposite side and patted down the area with my hand to feel a distinct lump near the pocket's seam. On closer inspection, I found the transmitter wedged into the join of the inner and outer layer of fabric. EL Shithead's hasty search of my pockets missed the tiny object. This discovery generated an immense amount of relief for us.

With the module attached to my ear and the small pad extended to my temple, transmission and reception of brain signals became possible. I felt rejuvenated.

"Now, we'll see where dear, old Happydoo is. I just hope they haven't discovered his presence yet."

The signals, transmitted from my cerebral cortex, cyber-spaced outward through the building, on a code-dedicated electromagnetic wave to the android's processor-receiver. I let it send for a full minute—no response.

"Maybe he's not in a position to answer," said Freda.

"I'll leave it for a few minutes and then try again."

A few moments later, I tried again. This time a definite click resounded in my brain. The android's system had activated to store the message. For a moment, unused to performing this type of contact, confusion overwhelmed me and I hesitated. Freda grabbed my shoulders.

"Leave a message for him. You've reached his recorder."

My confusion vanished. "Happydoo? I know you are in the building somewhere. Freda and I are locked in a room—at a guess, I would say on the third floor. There is a force-field keeping us trapped. Please try to help us escape. Be careful and don't give yourself away."

There remained nothing more to do but exercise our patience. I lost all notion of time.

"Can you remember how long it's been since they brought me in here?"

Freda huddled close to me for comfort.

"It must be an hour or two at the least."

I gave it some thought. "The transporter dropped us off in the alleyway adjacent to the building at about 1730 hours, which made the present time to be close to 1900 hours."

While I deliberated, the entrance force-field retracted, and Pin-stripe stood there.

"Grub's up."

He held out plates of steaming food to us—behind him stood Ugly-one with a scowl on his face.

"Thank your lucky stars, Conroy. The boss feels you need to keep up your strength. If it was me, you'd be starving to death," said Ugly-one.

Pin-stripe added a bit of dry humor.

"Don't read anything into it—he's just fattening you both up for the kill."

"You shitheads are so fucking hilarious," I mumbled.

Pin-stripe quipped, "Don't worry. It's a one-way trip for the two of you. It'll soon be over."

"Tell your moronic master, I would like to speak to him."

"Not tonight, Conroy. He may find time tomorrow, but I wouldn't bank on it."

The shitheads withdrew and the force-field closed with a resounding crack.

Freda and I sat on our bums and picked at the stew. It wasn't too bad, considering our prisoner status. While still involved with my bio-molecular education at the Institute of Learning, worse grub had passed my lips.

Freda did not look anywhere near as glam as she usually did. The peroxide streaked hair stood out at different angles, bunched up on one side of her head, caused by sleeping on the floor. Her lips, void of lipstick and her face, a whiter shade of pale, gave her the appearance of a ghost.

She picked up on my occasional glance at her condition and frowned.

"I must look a dreadful sight. I've lost track of how long I've been here, and they haven't provided me with anything to fix my hair or face. The apartment provided a little comfort because they locked me in the master suite."

"You look beautiful considering the situation."

She appeared pacified for the moment, but I could see signs of her self-consciousness. We finished the food and set the plates near the door. A long night lay ahead and I wondered about Happydoo and the message. He remained our only hope.

An absence of blankets and pillows made bedding down a little difficult. Lying on the cold, hard floor became uncomfortable after a while, so I tried to sit with my back against the wall. Freda moved over to me and cuddled up as I placed an arm around her. My mind still slinked back to thoughts of Carla, but there would be nothing lost by a show of affection for Freda. A week ago we shared very intimate moments, yet it all seemed vague to me now.

About an hour later, I fell asleep with Freda's head on my shoulder and dreamed about Carla. She appeared in a nightgown and beckoned me toward my cubicle on the Andromeda. I could sense the familiarity of the spacecraft environment as she climbed into the sleeping pod and beckoned for me to follow. I lay beside her and as our lips touched, a sharp crackle invaded the fantasy and caused the dream to vanish.

My eyes shot open. It took a moment to focus on the entrance and comprehend the retraction of the force-field. In the doorway, stood a form. I cringed—my captors had returned.

∞∞

Thirty-One

A Sight for Sore Eyes

My eyes struggled to focus on the figure at the room's entrance. I braced myself for a kick and raised my arm to protect Freda. Could the Ugly-one have returned to satisfy his violent nature?

'Are you okay, Master Beckett?'

Instant relief washed away the dread of an attack. The android moved into the room and hovered over us.

"Am I ever grateful to see you, Happydoo."

'I am happy to be of assistance, Master Beckett. My intervention would have come earlier, but I waited for the men to retire for the night.'

Freda woke up. "What's happening," she asked.

The presence of the android attracted her attention.

"Happydoo—you are a sight for sore eyes."

'I'm happy to be of help, Miss Freda.'

"Do you know where those two shitheads are, Happydoo?"

'They are asleep in a room at the end of this corridor, Master Beckett. There is no sign of Dr. Nassir. I worked around the security system until I found the main panel which controls the surveillance cameras and alarms and neutralized it, so we are free to go.'

"Do you know if there is a research facility or laboratory in the building?"

'There is such a room at the other end of the corridor. I think it might be where Dr. Nassir is doing research work—perhaps trying to unravel your father's discovery, Master Beckett.'

"Let's get out of here, then. Take us to the lab first. I want see what's in there."

'I am happy to do that for you, Master Beckett.'

I helped Freda stand as we both felt stiffness in our joints.

"What other rooms are there?"

'The other rooms are all empty, Master Beckett. The second floor is a factory and the

ground floor has finished-product and spare-parts for the equipment. The lab seems to be the admin office for the enterprise.'

The corridor, across to the opposite end of the building, exposed several empty rooms. Happydoo led the way to the last room, bigger than the rest, with window-view to the outside of the industrial complex. The desk in one corner attracted my attention. We needed to find something to tie Nassir to this place.

"See if you can find any info-vials while I check the drawers of this desk."

Freda and Happydoo searched the desk-processor. Several info-vials in a catalogued, vial-storage tray behind the quantum drive came to light and I pocketed all of them.

While we continued to search the concealed lights in the room dipped to a lesser lux-factor and an alarm outside the building sounded.

Freda ran to the window to look into the yard below.

"I thought the alarms had been de-activated."

'The internal alarms are offline. That is an external alarm and must exist on another circuit, Miss Freda."

"We have to get out of here," I said.

Happydoo moved to the window and scanned the perimeter.

'There is a group of five people moving toward the front door, Master Beckett.'

I peeped around the corner of the lab entrance to be greeted by the sight of Pin-stripe and Ugly-one on the move toward our cell. When they found it empty Pin-stripe yelled at his partner, who endorsed our escape with a flow of profanity and curses.

The two shitheads turned and charged toward the stairway that led to the second level, below us. They headed toward the room adjacent to the factory floor which contained the remote weapons. I could not comprehend the identity of the insurgent force—friend or foe, it complicated matters.

I turned to the android. "Is there any other way out?"

Happydoo cocked his head to one side.

'There is no way out from this level, other than those steps, Master Beckett. I suggest we remain here and see what happens.'

Once again, Happydoo made sense of things. We slipped back into the lab-office where I continued to search the drawers for vials. Freda stood at the doorway and kept an eye on the corridor.

I cursed the circumstances. Despite Freda's rescue our plight appeared to be far from over. Pin-stripe and Ugly-one needed to be neutralized—and what group now approached the building? How would it be possible to escape unnoticed? The questions rattled around in my head but no quick solutions came to mind.

A minor explosion erupted downstairs at the front entrance. The anonymous group must have blown the force-field. For a few moments we waited—then an all-out war broke out in the factory below us.

The sharp swish of laser-fire filled the building, followed by heavy impacts and mini explosions. It continued for several minutes, punctuated by an occasional lull, as the combatants tried to reposition themselves, or obtain clearer firing lanes. To end the exchange a huge explosion shook the floor and walls of the factory—I guessed the force-field between the factory floor and the office must have been breached.

The acrid smell of smoke permeated to the third floor and we wondered about Pin-stripe and Ugly-one. A sudden yell, followed by a final volley of laser-fire, brought an eerie quiet over the area.

A few minutes later, three armed combatants with body armor and field-masks, appeared at the top of the stairs on our floor. They swept the landing and looked into each room—a well-coordinated search with lasers at the ready.

With no avenue of escape we backed into the lab and waited for them to reach us. Two of the group burst into the room with lasers trained at our chests and stopped. A third person entered to bring the confrontation to its final phase—I hoped we would not be shot down like rabid dogs.

The third combatant lowered the laser and signaled to the others to do the same. A sense of relief overcame me as this appeared to be a military operation. The third combatant lifted off the field-mask—Sylvia Duke.

I didn't know whether to relax or be concerned. She cast a wary eye over us.

"We meet again, Mr. Conroy. Why am I not surprised?"

"On the contrary, Agent Duke. You should have expected to see me here."

"I can't say I'm enchanted by your presence, Mr. Conroy. What, if I may ask, are you and your companions doing here?"

"Following up a lead on Miss Banning which proved to be correct. Nassir locked her up here for a few days."

"Why didn't you go to the police?"

"We felt it would be best to leave the police out of it, for now."

"Do you know who those dead people on the factory floor are?"

"They are members of the WGF security team." I said.

There seemed no reason to keep Duke in the dark so I told her the whole story. She listened with controlled patience until I ran out of words.

"You and your companions will accompany us to Headquarters. My superior will want to find out more about the research material."

She motioned to the other two agents who removed zip-ties from their pockets and proceeded to secure our hands. My anger at our arrest vented itself.

"What are you doing, Duke? We've been victims of abduction and imprisonment by those two morons who work for Dr. Nassir. We aren't criminals."

"Those two morons are no more," she said. "For all I know you could have been in league with them."

She turned and walked back along the corridor. The other two agents jostled the three of us through the office entrance and we followed in Duke's wake. The news about the fate of Pin-stripe and Ugly-one pleased me no end, but I did not look forward to further interrogation by the EIA.

Duke must have conferred with Jameson somewhere along the line. The EIA should know my position on the vial by now and my quest to find Freda. The real question, however—did they have an agenda of their own, besides helping the WGF reclaim the discovery?

We followed Duke down the steps to the second floor and entered the smaller office. The site of Pin-stripe and Ugly-one, lying face down on the ground with huge laser-burn marks, did little to raise my spirits.

Freda could not look at them. Happydoo seemed untouched by the scene as we passed through to the factory floor. It became evident by the damaged equipment, and general destruction of the control panel, that HMC would not resume its manufacture of products in the near future, if at all.

I checked on the time—0100 hours am. There would be nothing more to accomplish at the factory and at best, we would share a cell at the EIA for the remainder of the night, until dawn.

∞∞

Thirty-Two

The Assistant Director

An official FIA transporter carried us, under the watchful eyes of our new captors, to agency headquarters. A cell allocation, which we hoped to be a temporary measure, accommodated the three of us with a squeeze.

Duke asked if we required any refreshment. Freda declined but I accepted a mug of cafteen, to wash away the sour taste of all the stress, in my mouth.

A young operative processed our incarceration documents and locked us in for the remainder of the night.

Adrenaline kept me awake while, within minutes, Freda fell asleep. The android sat in a corner to conserve energy—its system would require a recharge within six hours.

At about 0430 hours sleep came to me, and once again, my subconscious surfaced to lead me into a universe of fantasy and make-believe. A while later, a hand shook my shoulder to wake me from dreamland and my eyes opened to see Happydoo's two blue-colored, artificial orbs.

'Wake up, Master Beckett, wake up. We are being told to make ready for a meeting with the EIA Director.'

Freda woke at the same time and looked around her, confused.

"I need to pee," she said.

We accompanied an agent down a hallway to the ablution quarters. Happydoo remained outside while Freda and I saw to our physical needs.

In desperate need of a wash, I decide to forego a demisting in the ablution chamber as there appeared to be no auto-dress fabricator. A clean face and hands did, however, raise my spirits.

The same young operative escorted us via a verticap to the fourteenth floor. A trek along the hallway ended outside the office of Duke's superior, the agency's assistant director. The name on the holographic sign read: Thomas. M. Mendez. The escort spoke through a CCT to announce our arrival and a voice boomed out above our heads. *'Please enter. Your clearance is recognized.'*

The force-field retracted and the escort led us past an attractive female android to another doorway, through which we passed into the director's office. Behind a desk in the middle of the room sat the assistant director and opposite him, Sylvia Duke. Our entrance interrupted their conversation and they stared at us with a measure of malevolence.

Director Mendez remained seated and motioned us to sit in the chairs, which our escort pulled up from their floor niches. His intelligent eyes bore into mine, perhaps in an attempt to gage the depth of my resolve to withhold the information he wanted. I stared back in defiance at their smug faces and hoped to convey an image of one who would not be intimidated.

"Beckett Conroy, Padraig Conroy's son," he barked. It sounded more like a statement than a question.

"I knew your late father from past research security meetings."

This seemed to be a positive sign, but the perception dispelled in a puff of political smoke.

"We could never see eye to eye about security issues regarding the release of bio-molecular and genetic information to the general public."

My late father's knack of pissing off the wrong people appeared to include the big wigs in the NWEIA—this didn't surprise me.

"My father knew the dangers of keeping certain secrets from the public".

The director narrowed his eyes and observed me with repugnance—there would be no buddies made here.

"What do you know about the vial containing the information of his latest discovery?"

The pompous idiot already knew the answer to his stupid question. "Nothing more than you do, sir."

"You deny any knowledge of the vial's contents? I understand you are a level four geneticist—is that correct?"

I decided to remain as polite as possible under the circumstances.

"That is correct, sir. I had the vial in my possession for the shortest possible time before it was taken from me by the WGF security team."

Mendez gave a terse nod. "Jameson and Sutton have told me as much. I must warn you this has become EIA business. If I find out you have located the research information without informing us, the book will be thrown at you, is that clear?"

I still had some argument left in me. "But what about Miss Banning? Nassir's criminals abducted her and we need to find him."

"Nassir does not appear to have the research material and is of no use to us. I am going to be lenient on you and let you all go for the time being. We have leads to follow up, and if they prove to be of no use, then you and I will talk about the clue your father left."

I decided not to push the envelope any further. The assistant director wanted to have it his way. If anything, I felt an obligation to carry on the search in the hope of a discovery but Mendez would rot in hell before I ever revealed anything to him.

Mendez dismissed us. Throughout the entire interview Sylvia Duke sat with a smirk on her face and it became an effort for me to restrain myself from retaliatory measures. I guess the idiot wanted me to try, so she could have me locked up for assault. No way would I give her that opportunity.

∞∞

Thirty-Three

Freda's Discovery

The journey back to the Orion provoked little conversation from Freda or Happydoo, who seldom offered conversation, even under normal circumstances.

The thought of fresh clothes, a meal and a strong drink provided some relaxation, to ease trauma-filled memories of the night's long saga. I needed time to think. Jameson and Sutton might try to make contact to find out what happened to Lapinski and his men. There needed to be a clear-cut strategy to find out where Nassir might be in hiding. For the time being, no further consideration would be given to Mendez's threats.

Thoughts of Carla still distressed me. I needed to follow up on her and obtain some clarity with regard to our relationship. Closure would be necessary if she no longer wanted to pursue our connection.

The hotel foyer, buzzed with patrons. A line of people attempted to secure room reservations as we headed for the verticap. It felt good to be out of the EIA's line of fire, and the harassment of Nassir's goons. Uncle Sid appeared to have gone somewhere but left no message for us. I wanted to share the good news about Freda's rescue. It could wait.

My disposition bordered on lightheartedness, vested in the prospect of a cleanup and a strong whiskey. I told Freda we would meet at the bar lounge in an hour—Happydoo made straight for the charge booth and left me to enjoy a demisting in the ablution chamber.

The feel of soft suds, and soapy-mist around me could be described as pure heaven. I stepped up to the auto-dress fabricator and ordered a new suit, a new color—purple. The nano-fabric felt good against my skin and a quick examination in the mirror exposed my occasional tendency to vanity.

With a casual, "See you later," directed at the charge booth, I left the room for the bar.

*

Freda sat at the counter with a drink in hand. She looked quite stunning in a tight, black and white, nano-outfit which sported a swirling star-galaxy pattern.

Her hair, set in its normal style, contrasted with the silky-white skin and blood-red lips. We looked at each other for a moment and then laughed at our combined displays of amazement.

With my appraisal complete I settled beside her.

"You look absolutely great, Freda."

"Quite a change from last night, isn't it? You look very dapper and desirable yourself."

I Blushed and allowed my ego to soar to a new height. Where would this line of compliment-ing take us? I thought of the night we ended up in bed together and my pulse quickened.

We both ordered a bar meal to settle the first primal appetite, and then consumed some more whiskey to prepare the groundwork for the second greatest instinct—sex.

Several hours later, with Freda in the bed beside me, I felt gratified and I reflected on the act. It seemed even better than the first time.

"I'm beginning to enjoy these little excursions," I said.

"Don't forget, we agreed—neither of us is ready for any sort of long-term commitment, yet."

I heard a hint of sarcasm in her tone but decided not to take the bait.

"Agreed, but until such time I could get used to the 'arrangement,' if that's what it could be called." I answered.

She eyed me with a look of amusement. "I see it as being on a need basis and you can consider it a privilege—I have no other such 'agreement with any other man."

The thought of Carla still bothered my shaky sense of ethics which controlled all my personal commitments to the opposite sex. The whiskey, however, spoke with great wisdom and advised me to take my pleasures while still unattached.

Freda propped herself up on an elbow.

"With that out of the way, I can now tell you what I discovered before having lunch today." She had my attention.

"While imprisoned at Nassir's factory, I had some time to think. It's a strange thing your father did—I mean, in his initial attempt to hide the info-vial."

"Go on," I said. "What aspect of it?"

"He used Happydoo to hide the vial and then erased the memory from the android's processor."

"Yeah."

"I studied a little about AI processor memories when I worked at the WGF. Your dad and I attended the seminar together—being with him for the day increased my admiration, not only of his work but of him as a person. One of the things we learned was an application for hiding data in the recycle bin of a processor to avoid it from being detected in a memory sweep. Generally, only AI engineers would know this."

"I don't think I'm getting the point—"

She gave me a soft punch on the shoulder. "If you stop interrupting I'll get to my point."

"Sorry, please continue."

She smiled. "Your father appeared extremely cautious about the possibility of others getting their hands on his discovery. I am willing to bet he committed the entirety of his research to the recycle bin of the android's processor for protection. Not even Happydoo would know it was there."

Suddenly my interest perked up and recalled the lines of the clue, which I now remembered by heart. It all fell into place:

In a time long ago he died in a fall
Looking for eggs in the nest.
The vial is important but in the end
Your valet will pass the test.

I looked at Freda in astonishment. "I've been reading the clue incorrectly all along. I assumed the line, referring to 'my valet passing the test' meant Happydoo's rock-climbing ability, but it's possible my father was referring to the research having been stored in the android's processor."

"Maybe, the vial provided a sort of decoy for those who would try to steal it," she said.

I sat up on the bed. "Assuming it's there and protected, how would we gain access to it?"

"There will be a password required for entry. All we have to do is figure out what it is."

"So, if I understand this correctly, the recycle bin is normally accessible to any programmer, but there is a part of it where secret information can be stored under a password?"

"You are such a smart cookie, Beckett." She leaned over and kissed me on the cheek.

My immediate gut feeling agreed with her hypothesis. If my dad suspected the info could fall into undesirable hands, he might just as well have committed it to the only place he knew I might find it—his valet. It made sense to me.

Shifting my ass off the bed I moved to the ablution chamber.

"Let's get dressed and pay Happydoo a visit."

∞∞

Thirty-Four

We Pay the Lawyer a Visit

Back in my room we experienced a certain amount of frustration with our new mission. Under a flap of synthetic skin on Happydoo's back, access could be gained to the android program control panel. This feature allowed programmers a quick way to make selective changes in the field.

I tried several passwords, which included the names of places and dates but none of them would work. Freda made several suggestions, all to no avail.

After thirty minutes I threw in the towel and fell back onto my bed, defeated.

"I guess I just didn't know my father well enough."

Happydoo tilted his head and screwed up his synthetic eyebrows.

'Have you tried your mother's name, Master Beckett?' Master Padraig often talked about her.'

I sat up and typed in my mom's name. A small green light blinked at me and the screen lit up, to display a line of numbers—the android serial number allotted to my valet.

"Great work, Happydoo. You know so much more than I do, about my father, I mean."

The android did his classic pirouette and stomp of the foot routine. Freda and I both laughed and the tension in the room dissipated.

Freda went to work and looked through a long list of recycled items.

"This could be it," she said. "I am transferring a file back to the active memory of the main processor."

Freda amazed me. She sometimes came across as a bit of an airhead, but I soon realized not to judge the book by its cover. Her knowledge of AI processes outstripped my own by miles and she possessed a good understanding of computer systems. Any opinion I previously held about the bipolar disorder problem became overshadowed by her present contribution.

Finally she closed the flap and Happydoo resumed a normal stance, his face a picture of concentration.

'I am accessing the passive memory now, Master Beckett. Please give me a moment to set up the voice protocol. There is a message from your father in this file.'

I hugged Freda. But for her perseverance we would still be hunting down information as to the whereabouts of the research.

My father, once again, spoke to us from the grave.

'Hello, again, Beckett. Sorry for all the clandestine actions leading up to this crucial moment. I have known for some time that different parties are trying to grab the success of this discovery. I have tried to lay false leads for them. You will have discovered the info-vial at Eagle's Nest does not have the final research, or the truth of what my breakthrough entails. My guess is that the info-vial is already in the hands of the en-

emy—it will do them little good. The recycle bin of Happydoo's processor has been the only hiding place, hopefully, where no one else has thought to look. If you are listening to this message it means you were smart enough to work it out.

My mind danced an uncertain jig at the sound of my dad's words. For a moment the occasion overwhelmed me. I asked Happydoo to stop the recording for a moment so I could stem my yo-yo emotions. Freda put her arms around me, and I felt the wetness of tears as her cheek touched my neck. The unsettled emotion lasted for a couple of minutes and when it passed I nodded at Happydoo to continue.

"The truth is greater than the WGF realizes. Only Dr. Nassir, my colleague in Bio-molecular Genetics and Neuroscience, knows the extent of the discovery, but he doesn't know the secret. It goes far beyond the genetics of DNA and telomeres. What I have discovered is a way to transfer consciousness from one body to another.

'As you can imagine, this opens a whole new perspective on longevity. In fact it borders on

A-mortality, or immortality, as the more religious-minded might call it. It means we will be able to transfer the consciousness of a dying person to a host body of our choosing. All my research on the scientific detail can be found under "Host" in the recycle bin.

I am busy looking for a small premises in Dirac Heights, a light-industrial area in the north of Quantum City, where I will establish a satellite laboratory. My lawyer, Tom Callus, will tell you where it is.

'The entrance code to enter will be 'consciousness.' You will discover more about the host process when you study the details and visit the lab. There you will find an experiment set up and waiting. The first part will be accomplished. I leave it up to you to complete it by following the instructions. Good luck, son.'

I paced around the room in an effort to absorb the enormity and scope of my dad's discovery. Freda glanced at me with expectation.

"What are we going to do, Beck?"

"I guess we'll be paying the lawyer a visit."

A quick glance at the time confirmed the need to act urgently—1520 hours. The lawyer should be at his offices. My intuition told me Nassir would turn over every stone to find my father's final research.

He would know by now that the vial, presently in the WGF's possession, contained no solutions. He would also know about the demise of his two shitheads and realize that the EIA and WGF would conduct a search for him.

Freda wrapped her arms around my waist. "What are we going to do about Nassir?"

"It may be a fortuitous resolution to the problem if the EIA caught up with him but not at the expense of them gaining any more information regarding the discovery. The EIA cannot be ruled out as players in this whole saga of events."

Happydoo, hopeful to be included in the conversation, made an astute comment. *'Assistant Director Mendez appeared to be a man with an agenda—a man who wanted to line his own pockets, Master Beckett.'*

The course of direction became clear.

"Let's get going. The sooner we speak to the lawyer, the better."

The lawyer's office on the corner of Feynman and Green streets presented an ominous statement of misgiving for us. The secretary, a lady in her fifties, looked up from a holographic filing system and smiled.

"Mr. Callas had a visitor earlier this morning and after a short conversation in his office, the visitor left. An hour later Mr. Callas left saying he would be back first thing tomorrow—is there anything I can help you with, Mr. Conroy?"

"Can you tell us who the visitor was?"

"I'm sorry, Mr. Conroy. All I can tell you is that the person is an old client."

"Dr. Nassir?"

The secretary looked surprised. "Again, I'm sorry I cannot reveal any information."

"I need to speak with Mr. Callas urgently."

"I'll see if I can get him on the omninet," she replied.

After a minute she gave up. "He's not answering."

"If you give me his address, I'll get on a magnotrain and go see him. It's to do with my late father's estate—a very important matter."

She looked suspiciously at me and then relented. "Very well. Please don't tell him I gave you the address. It's not really something he likes his client's to have."

∞∞

Thirty-Five

A Nasty Discovery

Callas lived in a Level 0 credit area. The ultra-modern, modular buildings looked a bit like a beanstalk with pods, which stuck out at all angles. Entire rooms could be changed at will whenever the owner felt the need for new décor. It took the sting out of renovation.

The magnotrain passed in silence beneath the Callas's abode and stopped at the closest verticap, which serviced a line of dwellings.

The names of resident families, serviced by the platform, could be seen on overhead screens. The lawyer's name appeared above the entrance of the first verticap.

The trip up to ground level took only a few seconds and we stepped out onto a landing, situated fifty meters above normal street level. A walkway led to the front entrance of the Callas's residence. A moment later an unobstructed entrance to the portico brought a sense of apprehension. The force-field had not been activated and I felt trepidation with regard to the lawyer's wellbeing. Nobody ever left their front door open.

We entered and stopped to listen for sounds of life but only the soft hum of energy, from the power service, greeted us.

I took the lead and walked into the adjacent room, a furnished lounge, neat and tidy, but empty of any human presence. An opaque graphene-glass divider separated the living-room from what I guessed to be the office. Vague shapes and forms could be seen through the glass. One such form looked much like someone in a chair at a desk.

"Mr. Callas—is that you?" I called.

My words fell on deaf ears. We moved around the corner of the divider to enter the office and our eyes confronted a chilling site—Tom Callas sat in his chair with both arms folded across his chest. A burn-hole occupied the center of his forehead, like an exotic stone.

The lawyer's eyes remained open but expressionless, and the once handsome face, now displayed a grimace of shock. Disaster followed his final interview, and there appeared little doubt in my mind as to the guilty party—Dr. Nassir.

Freda stifled a scream at the sight of the dead man. There would be no information gleaned from him.

"Nassir must have worked out part of my father's strategy. According to the message my dad left me, he and Nassir partnered on the same project."

Happydoo confirmed my suspicion of Nassir's involvement. *'Dr. Nassir worked closely with your father on the genetics of the longevity discovery, Master Beckett. He would know about the extension of human life through the strengthening of the DNA's telomeres. It is possible he might also have known about the research on consciousness transmission.'*

Freda raised her eyebrows. "All the more reason for Nassir to steal the research. He knew, probably from Padraig's general conversation, there had been a much greater breakthrough."

Her conclusion touched one of my investigative nerves.

"My father had probably confided certain things in Nassir with the intent of obtaining his help but then perhaps didn't need it."

The android, not to be outdone in the post mortem of rhymes and reasons, added its own observation.

'Master Padraig may have involved Dr. Nassir on the earlier research which would have been at the WGF laboratories, Master Beckett. When the progress escalated to actual experimentation the research must have been moved to Dirac Heights without Dr. Nassir's knowledge.'

Happydoo's reflection made good sense but whatever reason underpinned Nassir's actions, we only possessed half the equation—a partial address for the location of my father's lab.

"We cannot afford to be involved with this death in any way. There's too much to be done—for now. Finding the lab's location has top priority."

Freda looked doubtful. "How are we going to find it?"

"I don't know but I need a stiff drink. How about we find a pub and do some strategizing?"

There being nothing further to accomplish at the lawyer's home we left.

∞∞

Thirty-Six

Searching for My Father's Lab

After Happydoo researched the location of a public bar through the omninet, I asked him to find the nearest weapons provider.

"We need to arm ourselves before undertaking any potentially hazardous search for the lab."

We discovered a shop still open quite close to the bar. Both venues resided in close proximity to Dirac Heights.

The weapon vendor provided the general public with an array of stun lasers and other medium-powered weapons for personal protection. I chose the strongest of the stun lasers, a hand-held model which seemed a reasonable deterrent to any hostile attacker.

If fired at close quarters it could be lethal. The purchase went against my available credit and we left to make our way to the pub.

The liquor joint gave the general impression of a dive, but after a few drinks, the ambiance improved greatly. The problem of the lab's location generated a brisk discussion. Medical research facilities did not feature among any of the known categories of Dirac Heights; my father must have used some other business classification for the lab so we brain-stormed the possibilities.

I looked at the use of family names, birth months and years, anything to do with 'consciousness' or 'genetics,'. We finally settled on three potential sites: DNA Holdings on 31st Avenue; Livelonger, Ltd on 37th Avenue; and Thought-Select Enterprises on 42nd. There being no other probable names, I felt confident we would find it under one of the selections.

A magnotrain serviced the light industrial area and provided a circular route that covered the outskirts. Escalators covered every avenue, eighty-four in total, which made Thought-Select Enterprises on 42nd, the longest distance of the three, to travel.

"This might take us the entire night," Freda commented.

"We have to find it. No one else knows the details of the experiment, so if Nassir or the EIA have been there, they would not be able to resolve anything."

A short trek to the nearest magnotrain station took a few minutes. We disembarked at 31st Avenue, to search for our first prospect—DNA Holdings.

The escalators contained hordes of people and androids at the end of a dayshift, plus the incoming staff for the night. Androids, prohibited from staying on any industrial premises, garaged in double-stack warehouses on the outskirts of Dirac. Humans provided most of the supervision and programming for the myriad of robots employed in many of the plants.

We looked for a small premises, a rental from a larger concern, but none of us possessed any ideas as to what the lab would entail.

Happydoo spotted the holographic sign of DNA Holdings from a distance. The three-story building boasted a long line of workers, egressing the factory area, all who appeared to have completed their shift. As we drew closer the sign displayed the names of the owners in smaller letters beneath the acronym: Dennison, Nichols, and Anderson.

"This is definitely not the venue we are looking for," I said. "We should carry on with this escalator until we tie up with the magnotrain route again and continue on to 37th Avenue."

Freda and Happydoo concurred and we stayed on the escalator. Half an hour later, we picked up the magnotrain to disembark onto the escalator at 37th Avenue and Live-Longer Ltd finally made its appearance.

The premises sparked my interest. Situated on the corner of a larger building, the sign above a single door lit up a flight of steps that led to the second floor. My heart wanted to leap out of my chest. We ascended the stairs toward the force-field barrier.

"Although no proprietor name is advertised, everything looks right. The rest of the building appears to be old and out of use. I think we have found what we are looking for," I said.

Freda felt the same as I did. "This has to be it."

I pressed my thumb on the right-hand upright of the door jamb—an image of a keypad appeared and then typed in the word, 'consciousness' as per my dad's instructions. I waited and a moment later the force field retracted, to give us access to the room beyond. I felt a pang of delight.

"This is definitely the place."

With laser at the ready, I crept forward into the darkness of the interior followed by Freda and the android. Triggered by movement, a light turned on and illuminated a small reception office. The room did not appear to be used for its intended purpose. A table, with a few items of electronic gadgetry on it, stood against one wall.

'I am sensing a trace of cryogenic medium in the air, Master Beckett.'

"What sort of medium are you talking about?"

'Liquid nitrogen, commonly used in cryonics, Master Beckett.'

"Why on earth would my father be messing around with cryogenics?"

Freda looked hopeful. "He could have been using it for cadavers or cultures, maybe to do with his work on DNA."

'You're probably right, Freda. Of course, he would need to freeze things—I should have known that."

We approached a second room on our left. I crossed over the threshold which triggered another very bright, overhead light. My eyes momentarily blinded, caused me to trip over a body on the floor.

A woman in a white lab coat lay there in a pool of blood. I stepped backward with haste and let out a gasp of astonishment. After a moment my surprise passed and I knelt to feel the woman's jugular—she was dead.

To get a better look at her, Happydoo helped me roll the body over. The face looked familiar but my memory wouldn't compute.

"She hasn't been dead all that long. Her skin is still warm to the touch."

We all sensed a distinct atmosphere of unease. For the first time my eyes focused on the contents of the room.

One entire wall contained a bank of holographic platforms, all actively lit. An array of short distance antennas appeared to receive and transmit signals from equipment situated in various other parts of the room.

Lights blinked on and off in sequences and a main screen indicated status reports with system analysis, all in relation to some type of an experiment. A darkened glass panel in the adjacent wall caught my attention. Whatever the instruments monitored appeared to be situated in a chamber beyond the panel.

I looked through the glass but only a white, misty vapor could be seen. I turned back to the holo-platforms and scrutinized the system in an attempt to figure out what it represented.

The largest platform showed a hologram of a man's body, erect in a chamber with arms outspread. Other figures represented temperatures and pressure in the chamber—some readings flashed on and off almost faster than the eye could see while others blinked more slowly and changed values at certain time intervals.

I felt a sense of wonder, followed by a dread. Freda stood and stared, her eyes wide open and mouth agape. Happydoo screwed up his eyebrows in a frown.

'This appears to be Master Padraig's laboratory, Master Beckett.'

I couldn't contest the statement in any way—in my heart I knew it to be true. A phrase from the recycle-bin message my father left came to mind—'Host Bodies.' Did the chamber contain a 'host body' for the consciousness transmission experiment? I had not given much thought as to how a consciousness could be separated from the brain, or where it would be transferred to.

The whole exercise seemed like a fantastic dream but the concept made sense. My dad, not content with the mere extension of life, decided to set up an experiment to transfer the conscious mind to another body—incredibly thought provoking.

My mind returned to the woman who lay dead on the floor—I knew her from somewhere but the drawer to that particular 'filing-cabinet' in my mind would not materialize.

I turned to Freda and made a suggestion.

"Could you please check Happydoo's recycle bin again for information on 'host body'? I need to find out how to access the experiment."

Freda nodded and the android complied by turning his back so she could access the programmer's console. After a few minutes she managed to access the file for transfer to the android's active memory. Once Happydoo accessed it he converted it to sound and my dad's voice, once again, floated through the air.

'By now you should have accessed my laboratory in Dirac Heights. Do not be bewildered by the instruments. I have a detailed outline of what everything does and how it works. You will see a glass port in the adjacent wall, which will allow you to view the experiment within the chamber. This can only be possible when the chamber reaches ambient temperature and normal pressure, which will take at least an hour.'

∞∞

Thirty-Seven

Setting the Experiment into Motion

So far, My assumptions appeared to be correct. I motioned to the android to halt the recording.

"This is amazing! I wonder where he found a host for the experiment."

Freda fingered a peroxide-streaked lock of hair.

"He must be using some unfortunate person's cadaver."

I motioned toward the dead woman on the floor, "He obviously didn't work alone."

Happydoo took the silence to continue with the recording.

When the chamber has reached the optimal condition, the host should be in good shape. Once the host has been normalized, start the transfer of consciousness. This will take about three hours.

The directions in the file on 'normalizing the host' turned out to be very easy. "I'm going to start the procedure," I said.

Freda gave me a frightened stare. "Are you sure this should be done, Beckett?"

"I want to know if my father's discovery works. I'm willing to bet, up to this point he hasn't tried anything with a human host. I owe it to him—the details leading up to this breakthrough cost him his life."

Freda still looked mortified. "But does it have to be done now? What about Nassir—he must be around somewhere?"

"Fuck Nassir. He's just another goon trying to muscle in on the process. History could be made here tonight."

She looked doubtful but said no more. The directions seemed clear and I followed them and keyed in the relevant information to the master computer which governed the process.

Lights blinked on and off and a 'countdown' clock showed up on one of the holographic platforms. It started at sixty minutes. My heart raced in anticipation of observing the host body. I half hoped the experiment would fail because if it succeeded, the moral issues raised, would bring with them irreversible consequences.

*

Forty minutes later, with the countdown at twenty minutes to normalization of conditions in the chamber, my mind became consumed with the details of the consciousness transmission. Some of the detail went completely over my head and revealed my lack of knowledge with regard to quantum mechanics and related neuroscience. For a moment I cursed the childish pursuit of surfing which had robbed me of a better education.

In the meantime, Freda's attention, given her background in psychology, focused on the psychological aspects of consciousness transmission. She sat at a table in one corner and made notes on a small quantum tablet, a part of my father's entourage of equipment for the experiment. Happy-doo busied himself on the successive steps of the experiment. He committed them to his active memory and introduced omni-pedia solutions for the not-so-decipherable scientific language involved. This would, at a later time, go a long way to help us understand the science behind the phenomenon.

I felt some concern for the dead woman. My educated guess, of course, focused on Nassir as the culprit. He must have discovered the lab after torturing the lawyer and arrived to find her on site. Without the research, however, he couldn't make much of the experiment.

He would be back. The EIA also posed a danger and I fretted over the possibility that they might break in on us—they might accuse me of the unknown woman's murder.

My sole consolation rested in the fact of our unique knowledge—no one else had heard my dad's voice, to explain the details so explicitly. Nassir, however, knew of the lab and this made him the greatest danger to our present position.

I doubted the ability of the WGF to intervene. After Nassir's warehouse they possessed no further information to go on, other than to search for the errant doctor. I considered all these logistical positions but it hindered my study of the experiment at hand, so I tried to put them out of my mind.

A sound from beyond the lab caught my attention. I stopped my concentration on the experiment's details and listened. A moment later the sound came again to dispel any notion of an overactive imagination. The android also picked it up and cocked its head in the classical way.

Freda oblivious, continued with her thoughts on transmission-psychosis. She only took notice when I crept toward the lab entrance and stepped with care, over the dead body.

"What is it?" she whispered.

I indicated for her to be quiet and stopped at the lab entrance, to crane my neck and take a look into the passageway. The hallway light, operated by a motion sensor had not come on. The front entrance force-field could be seen and while I watched from my vantage point, it snapped back in sudden retraction. A single figure stood there, framed in the entrance by the dim light from the exterior holographic sign.

My eyes watered from eyestrain, in an attempt to recognize the person. When the man called out I managed to put a face to the voice..

∞∞

Thirty-Eight

An Unexpected Visitor

"Beckett Conroy?"

My hesitant response followed. "Dr. Nassir?"

I stepped around the corner of the entrance with laser at the ready. Nassir held both hands up to convey he carried no weapons.

"Beckett, I come in peace. We need to talk."

"After you tried to kill me, you want to talk?"

"I have never tried to kill you. However, if I had wanted to, you would be dead."

He made a good point. "So, what is it you want—one of your one-sided deals?"

Nassir remained quiet for a moment.

"I know what it must seem like to you, but I have only wanted to scare you into submission.

Perhaps that is a misstep on my part, and I apologize for what has gone before us."

"What is your point, Nassir?"

"My point is we both deserve something from your father's unique discovery. He wanted to pass the torch to you and I had assisted in the research that led to the discovery."

"My father obviously did not agree."

"That's true but there is a reason why he didn't want to share the discovery with me. Can I come in and talk to you?"

Since he appeared to have no weapons and no goons appeared to be present, I relented.

"Sure, come in but don't try anything funny."

Dr. Nassir entered the hallway and the force field snapped back into place. I stepped into the lab and allowed him to enter. His eyes widened when he saw the body of the unknown woman. He stepped over the corpse but did not take his eyes off it.

"Dr. Hinkley appears quite dead. What happened to her?" he asked.

"You're kidding me, Nassir. Are you saying you had nothing to do with this woman's murder?"

"Absolutely nothing, but I think I do know who the responsible party might be."

"Who do you think killed her, then?"

He pulled a small video-vial out of the top pocket of his nano-suit and handed it to me.

"I think you'll be interested to see what's on this recording. I removed it from the security camera after the lawyer, Tom Callas was killed. The killers were either sloppy or didn't know a camera had been installed in the room. I knew about it because Callas happened to deal with the legal issues of my drug-enhancement business."

Freda stepped forward. "You are a brute, Dr. Nassir. You had me imprisoned for several days in that hell-hole you call your business. Why should we believe anything you say?"

"Again, I apologize for the inconvenience we put you and Mr. Conroy through, Miss Banning, but I felt it necessary under the circumstances."

"What circumstances are you referring to, Nassir?" I waited with the video-vial in my hand.

"I needed leverage. You and your uncle were against me from our first meeting. It had never been my intention to harm Miss Banning and she would have been released after I had the necessary information."

I remained distrustful of Nassir's attempts to extend the olive branch. The tablet used by Freda to consolidate her thoughts on the experiment, still sat on the table, and it reminded me of the video-vial in my hand. I inserted the vial into the tablet and we waited. The two minutes that followed horrified us, as we witnessed the death of Tom Callas.

Three combatants with body armor and field masks, streamed into the lawyer's home office with lasers at the ready. The central figure told Callas not to resist—they wanted to ask some questions. Callas closed down the hologram on the platform before him and sat back in his chair. The voice of the speaker belonged to Sylvia Duke. She asked one question.

"Mr. Callas, tell me where Padraig Conroy's lab is located and the entrance code."

Callas responded. "That is privileged information."

Miss Duke leaned on the desk and glared at him.

"You are obstructing an EIA investigation, Mr. Callas. This is a matter of international security. If you don't tell me, I will have you shot for treason."

Callas looked from one combatant to the other. He clearly felt intimidated. A vein on his forehead became visible and perspiration bubbled up on the wrinkled brow. He looked like a cornered animal and perhaps a discretionary move on his part, led to him give Duke the address.

I would have thought the EIA had a code to govern the actions of their operatives in the field, but what we witnessed completely dispelled any notion of ethics. After receipt of the relevant information Sylvia Duke shot Callas at point blank range.

The lawyer flopped around in the confines of the large chair and then slumped over. One of the combatants walked around, raised the still form of the body and pushed it against the backrest. He then placed the arms out on the desk. I felt disgusted. My opinion of Sylvia Duke hit rock bottom.

Freda cried and even Nassir seemed moved. No good reason existed for Duke to have killed Tom Callas. Nassir broke the silence.

"It's very evident the EIA are acting on behalf of someone who wants to gain from your father's discovery. Their actions, in killing Callas, are a breach of operations protocol."

"They must have come straight here to verify the location and found this woman—what did you say her name was?"

"Dr. Hinkely. She is one of the city coroners."

Now I knew why her face appeared familiar. She facilitated my father's viewing at the morgue.

"You knew her? Did you know of her involvement with the A-Mortal research undertaking?" I asked.

Dr. Nassir sat in a lab chair. "No, I had no idea. I just know her from several symposiums we have jointly attended."

My mind began to race in an attempt to put all this information together.

"She had to be working with my father. He talked of using host bodies in the consciousness transmission project and would therefore require a human body for the experiment. She had the perfect job to supply the need."

Dr. Nassir nodded. "The EIA must have killed her, too."

"It doesn't quite make sense to me, yet. Why would they kill her? She would be the only person alive who might know something about the experiment."

Freda came up with a viable answer. "She would not know the details of the discovery, but only the practical application of the experiment. It seems as though she took it on herself to guard the process for some reason."

"You mean, because she couldn't lead them to the actual research material, they killed her?"

"It's possible. Perhaps we'll never know," said Freda.

I looked with suspicion at Dr. Nassir.

"The jury is still out on whether you are telling the truth, Nassir. What did you really want to achieve by this conversation?"

Dr. Nassir stepped around the chair and placed his hands on the backrest.

"Do you know your father's intensions for this experiment?"

"Not entirely—but I'm sure he needed to prove its viability for humans."

Nassir lifted his chin and stared down his long, pointed nose at me.

"I would say that is obvious, but do you know who he intended to use in the experiment and why?"

I looked up at the holographic platform that displayed the countdown process. Only four minutes remained to reach the optimum chamber condition before consciousness transmission.

"No—I can't say I follow what you are getting at."

A familiar sound broke the normal cacophony of noise in the lab. It came from the front entrance. The force-field retracted, de-activated from the outside. We all turned our heads to the lab entrance.

One reason for this came to mind—the EIA.

"Get behind something," I whispered.

The others dispersed toward the back end of the lab to look for a suitable place to take cover as I crept toward the lab entrance. Again, I stuck my head out and around the corner of the door to stare into the semi-darkness of the hallway.

Four figures stared back at me. I could make out the helmets and bulkiness of body armor, which confirmed my worst suspicions. The voice of Sylvia Duke rang out in the ensuing silence of our confrontation.

"Give it up, Conroy. We have you over a barrel."

∞∞

Thirty-Nine

The EIA Takes Over

"Are you going to kill me in cold blood like you killed Tom Callas?" I shouted.

Sylvia Duke appeared startled. "You know about the lawyer?"

"Yes I do—you were sloppy in your cowardly attack. There is video proof."

She laughed. "It doesn't matter. I have the law on my side. We are coming in, so don't try to put up any resistance."

She motioned for one of the combatants to move forward into the hallway and positioned herself at the entrance with laser raised. The overhead light, triggered by the movement, illuminated him nicely for me to fire one burst of laser fire.

My laser, set to maximum for the farthest distance and with the man only ten feet away, gave him no chance of withstanding the blast and it bowled him over backward. He lay where he had fallen.

Sylvia Duke reacted angrily. "What the fuck do you think you're doing, Conroy?"

Not waiting to make a reply, I searched the lab entrance for a force-field. When we first entered the lad proper, no field blocked our way, but whoever entered the lab before our arrival might not have reactivated it after leaving. Internal force fields did not automatically open or close.

The desperate search paid dividends—a keypad suddenly appeared on the side wall in response to my random finger jabs. To close off the entrance required the activation of one symbol, a red dot.

The force-field snapped into place and secured our safety for the moment. I could hear Duke's enraged voice on the other side of the barrier. She threatened all sorts of atrocities after they breached the field. Freda and Happydoo peered out at me from behind overturned tables, their eyes wide in astonishment.

Dr. Nassir popped his head out from behind a drum-like cylinder I assumed to be a part of the cryogenic process.

"Have you started the consciousness transmission yet?"

Still not sure of Nassir's overtures, I looked up at the control platform display to see a new countdown clock. It showed two hours and forty-seven minutes before the final stage of transmission would be completed.

I glanced across at the glass window of the chamber and noticed a change in the color of one of the two lights above the door—from red to green. The holo-display showed: 'Normalization for transmission activation achieved.' The experiment, already in the final phase, was now irreversible and I had no idea what would happen if I stopped it.

Happydoo must have read my mind. *'Don't stop the process, Master Beckett. You will destroy the transmission and consciousness will be lost.'*

"Does that answer your question, Nassir?"

He nodded. "What are we going to do?"

I looked stoically at him. "I honestly have no idea. They're going to blow the entrance force-field—all I can do is to make an attempt to prevent them from entering, but this stun laser is no match for their weaponry."

Freda spoke up from her hiding place. "Can't we try to negotiate with them?"

"There will be no negotiating with Duke. She knows we have what they want—they also know we have proof of the lawyer's murder."

Thoughts of action swirled in my mind, but I realized our future looked bleak. With some thought given to the details of the discovery, I imparted an instruction to the android.

"Happydoo—since the files of the break-through's details are stored in your processor, it's vital you try to escape. I will occupy the EIA so you can get away. If you manage to get out of here, find my uncle and tell him everything."

'I will be happy to do that for you, Master Beckett.'

With that settled, I overturned an unused table to use as a shield. The EIA's weapons could burn a hole through it but I felt determined to put up a fight. The table provided the best possibility of marginal protection while I took Sylvia Duke out.

I would be protected when they blew the force-field, but the position was in close enough proximity to deal a possible death blow to anyone who tried to enter. My short life reflected no history of bravery, but a sudden calm came over me as I steadied my nerves and focused my aim on the first person who would come through the door.

Interminable minutes passed as we waited for the blast. When it came, the force blew me and my table backwards by at least a meter. Dust and splinters of construction material flew everywhere and marred vision of the entrance. Apart from not being able to see anything, the table ended up on top of me and knocked the laser from my grasp.

I scratched around in the debris to find it. My hand clasped around the butt, and I yanked it upward to cover the entrance. The force of the explosion seemed to have taken our attackers by surprise.

I heard Duke's shrill voice. "You used too much explosive, you fucking idiots. There's probably nothing left inside."

One of the combatants offered an excuse about wrong explosive recognition codes, but Duke wasn't listening.

"Get the fuck in there and see if we still have something to work with."

A combatant groped his way through the dust and immediately tripped over the inert body of the unfortunate Dr. Hinkley. With him down, I fired directly at his field mask. He screamed and went silent. Duke and the other soldier barged in, firing their weapons indiscriminately.

They couldn't see much, due to the volume of dust still in the air. There appeared to be no intention, by our adversaries, that anyone should be left alive. I fired back and caught someone on the shoulder, the electric charge neutralized by body armor.

Happydoo chose the moment to make a break for the door. One of the combatants saw him, raised a heavy military laser-rifle and fired on the android at almost point blank range. I let go a hot beam at the soldier simultaneously, and he dropped to the ground.

With my worst fears realized I stared in shocked silence. Happydoo lay motionless on the ground with his head torn from the neck socket. One shoulder and arm lay separated from the tor-so beside his burned, mangled body. Smoke poured from a gaping hole where the shoulder socket used to be. I dropped my laser in aston-ishment—the android, my valet and friend was no more.

The sudden pang of grief equaled the pain experienced after my mother passed away. I gazed at the ruins and wished there could have been an alternative to all the carnage. Damn the EIA.

∞∞

Forty

Fighting Back

Duke kept her laser rifle pointed at my chest. I slowly stood with my hands in the air and eyes still riveted to the remains of the decimated android. She pulled off the field-mask and our eyes met. I had not hated anyone throughout my entire lifetime as I hated her at that moment.

Freda stepped out from her hiding place with hands clasped over her mouth in horror. She approached Happydoo's remains and knelt beside his decimated body. I knew her thoughts paralleled my own, her fondness for the android evident in the way she reached out a hesitant hand to touch its scorched torso.

All his antics, the pirouette and stomp of the foot when he felt he pleased someone, the 'I'm happy to do' whatever we asked—all the quirks and traits, lay in a ruin.

I thought of the processor. Happydoo's processor, situated in the titanium skull and protected from the most violent jolts, lay a few paces away. I wondered if it survived.

"Now you can see the futility of resistance, Conroy."

Duke stepped closer to me, the laser held high, still pointed at my head. I suspect your father might have committed the details of his research to the android's recycle bin. I hoped not to destroy it, but with a bit of luck the processor might still be intact."

I remained silent, too angry to speak.

Duke never took her eyes off me. In my periphery vision, I could make out the holographic display of the count-down clock—hours remaining: 02:00. She turned to the remaining soldier.

"Search him and the woman. Make sure they have no hidden weapons, then zip-tie their hands."

The combatant obeyed and came over to frisk me. I wondered about Nassir. It would seem Duke did not know of his presence. After zip-tying my hands behind my back, the soldier frisked Freda. The countdown clock displayed 01:56.

I stepped away from my position which caused Duke to follow me with the laser rifle.

"Where do you think you are going, Conroy?"

"I'm getting out of the way of your over-sized ego."

Duke smiled thinly. "Stay where you are, fucking smart-ass."

She moved toward the place where the android's head lay and without taking her eyes off me, knelt to feel around for the processor. The action caused her to turn away from the place where Nassir remained hidden. The other soldier busied himself with zip-tying Freda's hands.

I picked up a movement to the side of Duke's position. Nassir extended his one hand from the confines of his hiding place to grasp hold of the downed combatant's laser. He gradually pulled it toward his position and hoisted it to bear on Duke who by now held the android's processor in her hand. Then the fire-works started.

A laser blast caught Sylvia Duke between the shoulder blades. The body armor did not provide her full protection and the beam severed her spine into two pieces. The soldier dived for his laser which he set aside in order to zip-tie our hands, but his valiant effort came too late. Nassir stood and let him have the full force of the electric charge. The beam cut him in half. Within a few seconds both the soldiers and Sylvia Duke lay dead on the floor.

I stared at Dr. Nassir. He stood there with the laser pointed toward the ground.

"Now you can see I meant you and Miss Banning no real harm. I could cut you both down right now but I'm not a murderer. My offer to share the proceeds still stands."

With the wind taken out of my sails, there appeared to be nothing I could say to the contrary.

"You've made your point, Nassir."

We looked at the countdown clock: 01:43.

Freda came up with an idea. "We can take the processor out of the android's cranium and connect it to one of the computers. If it still works we should be able to recover all the research details."

I raised my zip-tied hands and indicated to be cut loose. One of the downed soldiers possessed a multi-tool on his belt which Nassir used to free me. In turn, I cut Freda loose.

"On the question of the research, Dr. Nassir, you were going to tell me why my father had cut you out of the project."

He picked up an overturned chair, set it back on its feet and sat.

"Your father and I were, at one time, quite good friends—until the death of your mother. Your mother's suicide upset your dad to the point of him not being able to function adequately at work for many months. During this time I carried most of the earlier research."

Nassir's explanation did little to attract me into his court.

"So, because you carried the earlier research for a while, you feel it grants the right to the final product?"

"Not the total credit, but yes, I feel I earned a right to share the proceeds. It's true your father deserves the credit for the final breakthrough in both the extension of the DNA telomere integrity and the consciousness transmission discoveries, but without my assistance the end result would not have been possible."

Somehow his answers did not seem to rise to the expected level of contribution required to ensure the ultimate success of my father's work. I felt Nassir might be overplaying his role.

"What did the other directors of the WGF know of the research? Dr. Sutton appeared ignorant of the consciousness transmission angle. He spoke only of the DNA Telomere project."

Nassir shrugged his shoulders. "We never told them we were working on consciousness transmission. It remained a secret between your dad and myself—we made a big deal about the DNA breakthrough only, because Jameson would have withdrawn permission. The budget allowed for one angle of research."

"And after my father cut you out of the project you never thought it fair to tell them about the consciousness breakthrough?"

"No. Jameson is a very ambitious man, and I feared if he discovered the full reality, our efforts would be swallowed up by WGF bureaucracy."

Nassir's words, in this instance, rang true. I wouldn't have trusted Jameson or Sutton with an empty piggybank let alone a discovery as huge as consciousness transfer.

Freda, in the meantime set about inspection of the derelict android's cranium to see how we could access the processor. She really possessed an aptitude for high-tech equipment. After removing a few clips, the entire quantum drive came away in her hands. She lifted it up to the light for inspection.

"I used to play with computers as a teenager—it kept me out of trouble. We can use the same system of particle-entangled connection your father employed with the experiment, to access the information on the processor and transfer it to the tablet."

With the mention of the experiment I looked up at the countdown clock: 00:20. In another twenty minutes the consciousness transmission would be complete and the chamber would be open to reveal its contents.

∞∞

Forty-One

Another Visitor

A mix of excitement and trepidation filled my thoughts. Would my dad's experiment be successful? What would we witness when the chamber door opened? These questions remained unanswered for quite a bit longer than anticipated. A complication none of us could ever have expected, materialized—a cough from someone at the lab entrance announced a foreign presence.

"It looks as though a war has taken place here."

I did a double take. The familiar voice belonged to Uncle Sid. He stood at the door and surveyed the carnage—he held a laser rifle, pointed at the floor. My heart jumped with joy to see him again. Freda shrieked in delight and dropped the android's processor on the tabletop in astonishment. Dr. Nassir stood there, mouth agape.

"You are a sight for sore eyes, Uncle Sid," I exclaimed.

Freda rushed over and threw her arms around him in a bear hug. Uncle Sid allowed Freda to hug for a few seconds and then pushed her away.

"I'm afraid I haven't come in a capacity that would please any of you." He lifted the gun and pointed it at Dr. Nassir.

"You were always a thorn in the Conroy flesh, Nassir. You tried so hard to wrench my brother's discovery from me but today is payback time."

A bolt of concentrated light shot out and hit Nassir on the shoulder. He spun around, grasped at his arm and slumped to his knees. My bewilderment followed, expressed with raised, open hands in a gesture of confusion.

"What the hell are you doing, Uncle Sid. Nassir may not be as guilty as you think he is."

"Shut up, Beckett. You know nothing about what has really been going on here."

The icy tone in my uncle's voice sent a chilling message. I didn't know this man.

"What exactly do you mean, Uncle Sid?"

"Dr. Nassir—he's not who he has been making himself out to be. He is partly responsible for your mother's death. All those years ago, when he first started working at the WGF, Nassir assisted with the telomere extension research. He and your father became good friends."

My response came with a measure of impatience.

"I know all this already—can you get to the point."

"The scumbag tried to come onto your mother one night at a WGF year-end party. He lured her into a room under false pretenses and tried to have his way with her."

Uncle Sid's words fell like bricks on glass. I turned to stare at Dr. Nassir's pale face while my uncle continued.

"Your father walked in on them and thought your mother had been fooling around. He never forgave her. She tried to explain her position but he wouldn't hear it."

Dr. Nassir recovered enough composure to speak.

"I didn't mean anything by my actions. I had been drinking heavily and tried to explain to your dad it had all been my fault, but Padraig wouldn't listen."

Uncle Sid exploded. "You're a lying bastard, Nassir. You secretly hoped the incident would break up their marriage so you could move in."

I couldn't believe my ears—my mother—involved in a scandal? Anger engulfed me and I advanced on Dr. Nassir who put his arms up to protect himself.

"Your uncle is lying. His version is just his opinion—it wasn't like that."

His words stopped me in my tracks. Who of the two, alluded to the truth? "You don't deny luring my mother into a room, Nassir. Why should I believe what you say?"

The neuroscientist dropped his protective stance.

"Perhaps you should ask your uncle what he's really doing here. He didn't come to save you and Miss Banning. He has his own agenda."

In my confusion I turned to face Uncle Sid. Freda stood like a statue and listened with astonishment as I faced off against him for the first time in my life. A sense of disillusionment gripped me.

"What agenda do you have in all this, Uncle Sid?"

For a moment he looked at the ground and then raised the laser, to point it at my chest. I heard a click as the synchrotron engaged. It sent a chill down my spine and my knees turned to jelly. What on earth had come over my uncle? He stared at me as though my presence meant nothing at all. Perspiration began to bubble on my brow and I took a step back.

"I have always treated you as my own son, Beckett. I love you more than your father ever did, however—"

He paused, whether for effect or lack of words, I do not know.

"This discovery is much bigger than the both of us. It constitutes a moral threat to every-one on the planet."

His philosophy sounded like a genetic tree-hug to me. I'd never known his personal morality to contain any such ethical obligation—at least we never spoke of such things.

"I never agreed with your father regarding the extension of human life by these means. Death is a part of life and has been since the beginning. Our evolution includes a time-limit for every sentient life form."

"What do you intend to do about it," I asked.

"I will destroy whatever is in that chamber and I will kill anyone who tries to stop me. That includes you, Beckett."

Again, my confusion reigned supreme.

"But you encouraged me to find the research and follow up on the legacy of my father's work."

"Only so I could put an end to it. Believe me, I mean what I say."

The wind died in my sails. I couldn't have disagreed with my uncle more. All my father's work over the past eighteen years would be lost if Sid Conroy continued on his path. The countdown clock showed 00:04—four minutes for the transfer to be finalized and the experiment would be complete.

My mind raced to think of a solution.

"You are prepared to kill me to prevent the experiment from being brought to the scientific world's attention?"

"Don't think for a moment the thought doesn't scare me, Beckett. But as I said, the impact of such an opportunity can only be negative—the sacrifice of your life, even mine if it must be, doesn't hold a candle to the moral carnage following in the wake of such a provision."

My uncle never showed a glimmer of interest in the moral questions of society in any of our previous discussions.   The real issue, I believe, came from the lips of Dr. Nassir.

"The truth, Beckett, lies in your uncle's relationship with your late mother."

Now, the road became rocky and my thoughts spun out of control—information overload.

"What are you saying, Nassir?"

Uncle Sid's face turned red. "Shut the fuck up, Nassir. If you say another word, I swear you'll be shot down like the dog you are."

Dr. Nassir raised his hands in front of his chest, looked at the ground and avoided eye contact with me. I boiled over.

"What about you and my mother, Uncle Sid? Tell me the truth."

He took a moment to compose himself.

"Your father never gave your mother the time of day. She had so much to bring to the relationship, but he never gave her the opportunity—the same thing he did to you. His work always took priority. She killed herself because of that selfish bastard."

"Did you love my mother, Uncle Sid?"

"Yes, I did. But it never became physical."

Enough said—I didn't want to hear any more.

A sudden 'click' noise from the experiment chamber put an end to further conversation and we all knew its significance. The lock on the experiment chamber's door disengaged. I glanced at the countdown clock—all zeros. The consciousness transmission now at one hundred percent transfer, awaited our observation of the results.

∞∞

Forty-Two

The Greatest Surprise of All

We all stood rooted to the spot like statues. A 'swish' of gas within the chamber reached our ears as the chamber door opened. A mist of remnant liquid nitrogen burn-off clouded the entrance and made it difficult to see into the confines of the resuscitation compartment.

Instinctively Dr. Nassir hobbled toward the door. Uncle Sid must have waited for the moment because he fired a burst of laser, which narrowly missed me and caught the neuro-scientist between the shoulder blades. Nassir went down in an explosion of sparks and smoke, like a felled oak tree. He lay very still and I believed him to be dead. Freda's face contorted in horror and a groan of disbelief escaped her lips.

I could not believe my eyes. How could such a dramatic change have come over my uncle? I looked around at the human carnage; the two soldiers and Duke lay close to one another with the remains of Happydoo between them. Closer to the lab door, lay the dead Dr. Hinkley. The body of the first soldier, stunned by a shot from my laser in the hallway might still be alive unless killed by Uncle Sid, on his way into the lab.

I turned to look at the chamber. The liquid-nitrogen burn-off still drifted out from the compartment, which made it difficult to see inside. The green light above the chamber entrance blinked continuously and demanded our immediate attention. My uncle raised the laser and pointed it at the center of the inner chamber. He made his intention obvious.

I could not allow him to destroy my father's work. Whatever my dad's shortcomings, the breakthrough still remained an important solution to humankind's dwindle of reproduction numbers. What did my uncle think would happen after another two hundred years of attrition? The New World Earth Administration should be the ones to decide on the morality of such a unique provision. Not him.

I stepped into the line of fire and decided to risk my life in one last effort to save the experiment.

"You will have to kill me before you do this senseless thing. Just think, Uncle Sid—this discovery could save the human race from extinction."

I knew the laser rifle to be set on a kill-mode and my life now hung in the balance. I risked everything on one last notion—my uncle would surely not kill his only surviving nephew. It would be the end of our bloodline.

Freda screamed out a warning. "No, Beckett. He's not himself——he will kill you. Don't throw your life away for this."

Uncle Sid shouted a confirmation of Freda's fears. "I mean what I said, Beckett—get out of the way."

I stood there, rooted to the spot, terrified out of my wits. My entire life passed before me in milliseconds and consolidated the inability of my body to obey my mind, which screamed to back off.

A moment later came the whoosh of intensified laser light and I prepared to die. I wished, in those final seconds my body could react and get me out of harm's way, but my muscles wouldn't budge. A moment later, the distinct sound of a laser strike on a body, reverberated in my eardrums and I waited for my imminent death, like a petrified tree. But nothing happened to me.

Then I saw my uncle topple forward and fall face down on the lab floor. The sound of sparks, like static over an ancient radio system, exploded from his back and a puff of white smoke floated upward toward the ceiling.

Freda uttered a high-pitched wail which ended abruptly in a sob and I remained motionless in the tyranny of the moment.

The smoke cleared enough for me to see a figure at the lab door with laser in hand, still pointed at the remains of my uncle's body.

Then the person spoke. "Are you okay, Beckett?"

I thought my own eyes had deceived me—the last person I expected to see—Carla.

She dropped the laser and leapt over the bodies. In the space of a few seconds she lunged into my arms and both of us almost ended up on the floor. She wound her arms around my neck and tears coursed over her flushed cheeks.

After I managed to regain a balance, we remained in tight embrace; me in unbelief and Carla in cherished relief. Freda's eyes opened wide in shock, her face a picture of disapproval, but she held her peace.

After a minute of silence, punctuated by an occasional sob from Carla, we remained in a state of suspended animation. Her face remained buried in my neck while I struggled to make sense of what had just happened.

My utter delight to see her again tempered the counter-emotion of my uncle's demise. He, the one who nurtured me through the problems of life found a stronger purpose than love, to end his life for—an ideology of confused morality, for which he would have sacrificed not only his own life, but mine as well.

Carla lifted her head and our eyes met. She closed her eyes and raised beautiful, soft red lips to meet my own in a kiss of urgent rediscovery and I knew all would be well.

Freda's folded arms and stare, which I observed in my periphery vision, sent its own message. I couldn't imagine what she felt at that moment because of her attachment to me, but my love for Carla went beyond any sexual arrangement.

My reverie vanished in an instant at the sound of movement behind me. Freda's face, focused on the chamber expressed an astonishment not before seen, as she covered her mouth with both hands.

I swiveled with Carla still in my arms and lifted her full body weight to do so. Visible, through wisps of cryogenic vapor and extended on a structure of titanium steel, a man emerged. The body, still too weak to function, flopped around on the supports. The apparition's eyes opened to stare in wonderment at its surroundings. I released Carla and took a step forward.

"Dad?"

The eyes held mine with a gaze of the drugged, but recognition registered in the glimmer of a half-smile. My father, pale but recalcitrant to the grip of death, had clawed his way back to life.

But how? His lifeless body, viewed in the mortuary, still remained imprinted on my mind. The police testified to his electrocution and consequent demise. The questions burst the banks of my curiosity and demanded immediate answers. For several, long moments I gazed in fascination at this unexpected resurrection. Carla and Freda, both in shock, remained silent.

"It worked! The experiment worked."

My sudden enthusiasm resounded throughout the walls and roof of the laboratory. With tears in my eyes, I moved to the extended support structure that held the pale being in its clutches and stared in childlike wonder at the face. I reached out with a hesitant hand and softly stroked a cheek with the back of my fingers. The feel of the skin still retained an intense cold from the cryonic process, but the chest moved with the breath of life.

Carla and Freda overcame their inertia and joined me in the process of scrutiny. I could see recognition spark as father's gray eyes moved from face to face.

"Welcome back to the land of the living, Dad," I said.

He responded with a voice barely above an audible whisper.

"Glad to be back, son."

∞∞

Forty-Three

A Hasty Exit

We removed all evidence of our presence from the lab. I made no effort to move any of the bodies; Mendez, from the NWEIA would no doubt follow up on his subordinate's work and treat the area as a crime scene. My father, who still spoke in a shaky whisper, recommended we all melt into the shadows for now.

"The EIA will come looking for their people. They already know about the lab and when the operatives don't report back, they'll be all over this place."

I had another realization. "Sylvia Duke might have been carrying a recorder which transmitted the live operation back to their HQ. We should get out as quickly as possible."

A thought crossed Carla's mind. "I doubt whether Mendez and Duke acted under their corporate authority—I don't think he would be too quick to lay claim to this lot."

Freda made a suggestion. "We can't go back to the Orion. They know we were staying there—I know a small B&B where we can hide out for a time."

"We had better get moving," said Carla.

Freda placed Happydoo's processor and the tablet into a backpack which had belonged to the late Dr. Hinkley. My father suggested I remove the important parts of the experiment, specifically the vial designed to house the consciousness during its transfer, plus the program that ran the entire process.

Dad felt his immediate interests would be best suited if he stayed out of sight for a time and when things cooled down he would assume a new identity. No one would expect him to be around as The Administration and the NWE central computer had already processed his record of death.

With regard to the breakthrough's future, he wanted to talk to me in private.

*

No further incidents hindered our departure from the lab. The boardinghouse, situated in an older area of Quantum City, suited our immediate purpose. My father, supported all the way from the lab, endured the arduous journey with patience and humor. For the benefit of the few people we came across on the magnotrain and escalators, we scolded him for the excess use of alcohol. Nobody took any real notice of us. To them we looked like a group of revelers, out for a night on the town.

Few patrons appeared to be in residence at the B&B, and the admittance clerk seemed to suffer from poor eyesight. Carla and I booked a single room as Mr. and Mrs. Fox while Freda and my dad reserved as Mr. Fox senior, who indulged in extensive travel with his daughter, Sonja. I couldn't help a quip about 'too many foxes spoiling the vine', which brought a smile from the clerk. We were all worn out from the day's events and headed straight to our respective rooms.

Freda wanted to stay with my dad to make sure he made it through the night, so she opted to keep an eye on him. I felt a tinge of guilt about Freda but she understood that our arrangement would only last until one, or both of us, found a lasting commitment. My obvious love for Carla, already a visible reality due to our embrace in the lab, told its own story—although hurt, she appeared to have gained an acceptance and adjusted her attitude.

My dad's plans for the success of the experiment could not have foreseen the intervention of his own brother and I knew Uncle Sid's death greatly upset him. He told us how Dr. Hinkley became involved in the experiment over a year ago, with the hope of a post-doctoral paper on the vision of consciousness-transfer and how it would help save the human race.

She used a 'synthetic human stage-dummy', pre-constructed in my dad's likeness, to fool the police in their investigation. After the 'body' transferred to the morgue, she falsified an autopsy report—Uncle Sid and I viewed the same 'prop'.

Meanwhile, my father, in the flesh, situated himself with Hinkley's help, in the chamber and underwent an 'instrumental and clinical death', while his consciousness transferred to a specially designed vial situated in the chamber.

Dr. Hinkley watched over the process of cryogenics until we discovered the location of the lab and arrived on the scene. My father wanted the resuscitation process, and continuance of the project, to be my decision—Padraig Conroy would have remained dead had I not agreed with Dr. Hinkley to proceed with the venture. She planned to pull the plug should I not want to go through with the experiment.

The saddest aspect of our new found freedom manifested in the loss of Happydoo. In our new room a charge booth in one corner reminded me of the android and it brought tears to my eyes.

The lateness of the hour left Carla and I yawning, but not too tired for the inevitable. The room came with a stocked mini-bar which, to my delight, retained a bottle of Supernova in its limited inventory. We sat on the loveseat at the B&B window and enjoyed a nightcap. The change in circumstance seemed like a dream—a fantasy from which I hoped there would be no waking up.

"Are you ready?" I asked.

"I have never been more ready," she answered.

We climbed into the bed, eyed each other out for a moment and then I reached out my hand to touch her cheek. She sensed my greatest need of the moment and allowed my approach as I pulled her toward me. Our body's met in a gentle sober manner of exploration until our heightened drives could wait no longer. We plunged into sensual delight and stayed there until sleep overtook us.

∞∞

Forty-Four

The Best Course of Action

The commitment with which Carla made love to me that night confirmed her complete release from the ghosts of the past.

In the morning we got ready for breakfast and made a quick visit to my father's room. Freda sat on the bed beside him and held a glass of water to his lips. She mopped his brow with a cloth and seemed cheerful after what must have been a long night for her. The night's rest did wonders for my dad. His color seemed a little on the pale side but greatly improved.

"How's our patient this morning?" I asked.

Freda gave a tired smile. "Apart from talking in his sleep a few times, he seems to have had a very peaceful night."

My father turned his head slowly to look at me.

"Thank you, son—for believing in me." His voice sounded weak but audible.

"Despite the issues of the past, I could never have denied you your life, Dad."

He managed a grin. "The past is gone and we both have the promise of a new start. I've been born again, given a second chance—an opportunity I would like to make full use of, to mend our relationship."

"I agree, however, there is much to discuss regarding the future."

We spoke again of the strategy with regard to the experiment and the laboratory. No one would know the truth, apart from the four of us.

I felt sure Mendez, Sylvia Duke's boss, would make some excuse or other to resolve the mission's failure. The WGF directors, Jameson and Sutton, would try to push the point of my involvement but they didn't have evidence to pursue it.

I could see my dad needed to sleep again so Carla and I went to the lounge for some breakfast. Freda knew what my father required nutrition-wise, to help him recover from his ordeal. She promised to see to his quick recovery with all available health supplements.

Despite the difference in age, Freda and my dad appeared to be attracted to one another. This growing relationship provided me with an advantage—I could share the responsibility of his recuperation. There were many questions with regard to his recollections, the period of the consciousness transfer for one, but it would have to wait. More important matters required our attention.

Carla and I sat in the small dining area. Our clasped hands made our deep devotion to one another evident to the few other patrons enjoying their breakfasts. Her beautiful eyes kept me in a trans-like state—the exquisite blond hair, which sparkled in the light, captivated my undivided attention, to the complete distraction of everything else around me.

It became difficult for me to concentrate on the tasks ahead under her steady, happy gaze. We both made significant discoveries about each other which resulted in a strong emotional bond and union of love. It drew us together into a single nucleus, a marriage of two contented hearts.

I drew a line. "Carla, honey—I need to know how you came to find us at the lab last night. I thought you had disappeared into the blue."

She smiled at the reference to her period of silence.

"When Sylvia Duke brought me back to the EIA office, I was taken through a debriefing with her and the boss, Mendez. They hauled me over the coals for getting involved with you—they said it had not been the plan and I had broken EIA protocol."

My anger at Duke and Mendez rekindled. "It's just as well Nassir killed Duke, because if I ever got the chance—"

Carla cut me off. "Forget about Duke. She's gone from this world. The truth is she played a large role in getting me employed as an agent after the death of my husband. For that I am grateful, however, she is the one who broke protocol."

I shifted in my seat and rubbed her forearm. "How do you mean?"

"I believe Mendez won her over when he discovered the enormity of the breakthrough. Jameson and Sutton of the WGF don't know about the consciousness transfer. As far as they knew, the discovery embraced only the extension of DNA telomeres."

My intrigue went up a notch. "Nassir mentioned the fact that the consciousness experiment had never been shared with them."

"Yes. Mendez, Duke, and I knew because of certain intel we were privy to."

It made sense. I wondered if the WGF's lack of knowledge would keep them satisfied. "So, how did you know we were at the lab?"

She licked her top lip in a delightful, sensual gesture and gave me the eye, accompanied by a coy smile.

"I came because I wanted to be with you, my Sweet."

I laughed at her little joke but the tone of her voice rang with conviction. "Sure thing, honey—but how did you know we were there?"

"I followed your progress from the first visit to the EIA office. I monitored Sylvia Duke's dedicated information-train. I knew about the murder of Tom Callas and your consequent journey to

Dirac Heights. The EIA were observing you all the way."

I felt a little foolish. "I guess I should have realized they might do that."

"Don't worry, sweetheart. I had you covered and I'm glad I acted when I did. I arrived after Nassir entered the building, and not knowing your uncle would become involved, I decided to allow Duke and her guys in first. My plan, to catch them in the act of confronting you, backfired when all the explosions and laser-firing started. Terrified they might have killed you, I made a decision to surprise Duke and take her down. As I approached the entrance, Sid Conroy, who never saw me at the time, arrived."

With that cleared up, I changed the subject.

"I think we might need to pay the police chief a visit. By now they would know about the death of Tom Callas and possibly even have found the carnage at the lab. I'm concerned they might think I killed the lawyer. The law firm's secretary will have no doubt told them about me wanting his address."

"But at least you can prove the murderers were the EIA. You still have the video-vial Nassir gave you."

I nodded. "Freda has it—it's still in the tablet we used for viewing. They can't prove who killed the EIA team, which only became necessary in self-defense, anyway."

Carla smirked. "Hmmm...I don't think the police will even know about the EIA team. I understand how the agency works. Mendez will have been to the lab to remove the bodies of Duke and her accomplices. He would not want the authorities to know the details of the investigation. It will become classified business—in the interests of international security and the dead will receive an honorable burial."

I felt some relief at Carla's explanation. "So, we can safely account for our involvement without being suspected of wrongdoing?"

"No one, other than us, has any proof of what happened at the lab. We have evidence of the Callas murder. The WGF have no proof you ever found the real information-vial and with Dr. Hinkley dead, no one can prove anything to do with your father's experiment."

I made up my mind. "We should run it past my dad first and then get down to the police station."

Back in my dad's room, I asked Freda, who caught a nap in our absence, if she wanted anything to eat. She declined and said a mug of cafteen from the wall-mounted beverage replicator sufficed for the moment. I guessed, in consideration of the past twenty-four hours, she might still be a little wound up.

Five minutes later my father woke and asked for another sip of water. When he saw us, a smile broke out on his face.

"I'm glad you're here. What have you decided to do?"

"Both Carla and I feel we should pay the police chief a visit and give him a version of what went down last night."

I related the contents of the earlier conversation at breakfast. My dad listened and then nodded his approval.

"It will be good for you to square it all away—particularly the business with our lawyer. After that you should go to the law firm and establish what will happen with your uncle's business. Tom Callas had a partner—Denis Fincham. He will be able to check on Sidney's will."

We left it at that. My father still needed a lot of rest and as yet, he had eaten nothing. Freda called a pharmaceutical outlet close by and asked for a host of special vitamins. She felt confident my father, given time, would recovery completely.

I needed to ask about her mental condition but didn't want to pry.

"Do you have any of your own medication left? Would you be able to get what you need from the pharmacy?"

She gave me an icy glare. "My normal prescription will be arriving with your dad's vitamin package, thank you."

I knew not to press her about how she felt. If anything, she had weathered the storm remarkably well. Carla looked at me quizzically, but held her peace.

∞∞

Forty-Five

The Quantum City Police Department

We left the room and caught the escalator to the magnotrain station. "What was that about?" Carla asked.

I told her about Freda's condition. "I had expected her to crack long before this but she has amazingly held her own."

"She's doing a wonderful job with your father."

"Absolutely. I think she's quite taken with him."

Carla smiled. "Oh I guarantee she's taken with him—smitten I would say."

We arrived at the police department forty minutes later. It made such a difference with Carla at my side. Her positive attitude took every opportunity to compliment me and lift my self-image whenever my conversation slipped into self-deprecation. I do have the tendency to come down on myself in favor of past failures.

The chief greeted us with cordiality.

"I remember your dad's case. Electrocution, if I'm correct?"

I nodded.

"And what brings you to see me today?" he asked.

I told him the story of our arrival back on Earth due to my father's death and the consequent harassment by Dr. Nassir. I mentioned the clue left me and how it turned out to only provide us with normal, known research.

The chief's eyes widened when he heard of the NWEIA's involvement. Carla, as an ex-agent-operative, could testify to the WGF's involvement in Lapinski's mission to grab the info-vial from us.

"What happened when they discovered the vial did not represent the whole discovery?"

There shared this information. "They conferred with the WGF, Drs. Jameson and Sutton, to get me to make a deal to share the information, if I finally managed to work out the location."

"Your point in sharing all this information with me is not quite evident. Can you elucidate on your motive? So far it seems to be a dispute over a discovery, the final research for which has not yet come to light."

"My motive is to inform on our involvement in this whole saga. We also do not want to be implicated in the death of Tom Callas."

A glimmer of understanding dawned in the chief's eyes.

"The lawyer reported missing this morning? We've sent an officer to his house half an hour ago. His secretary called to say he hadn't been answering his omninet com. She feared something might have happened to him."

They say timing is everything. The buzz of the chief's own com took the chief's attention and he motioned for us to wait while he answered. His eyes seemed to grow in size as the caller related an urgent message. Then just as quickly he calmed and told the caller he already knew of the incident.

"That was the officer I sent up to the Callas residence. He confirms the death—now please tell me how you knew about this."

I placed the video-vial, removed from the camera in the Callas home-office, on the desk.

"You may want to view this. It explains the circumstance of the lawyer's death."

The chief inserted the vial into a processor and the hologram of the vicious attack by the EIA team displayed on the platform. When the video came to an end, he rubbed his eyes vigorously with both hands. I explained how the vial came into our possession and he touched a key on the desk-pad, to dictate some notes.

In conclusion, I shared the attack on the lab by the EIA and the consequent deaths of Dr. Nassir and Uncle Sid with one omission, the result of the experiment.

"Thank you for your testimony. I would advise you not to leave the city until we can put all this to rest. I doubt if anything will come of the EIA's involvement. I know how they work—any mistakes with consequent collateral damage are simply contingencies. It all happens in the interests of national security."

Carla and I left the police department with the reasonable hope of our involvement being seen as an incidental part of the EIA's investigation. My hope of this vested itself in Mendez's discovery that there was no further information with regards to the final research. The equipment in the lab would show an experiment still in the planning stage, but an endeavor which yielded no result.

Our next port of call had to be a visit to the lawyer's office.

∞∞

Forty-Six

The Lawyer's Offices

The distraught secretary greeted us with handkerchief in hand.

"We have just received terrible news," she said.

I acted dumb and asked her what had happened.

"Mr. Callas has been murdered." She burst out in a sob. "The police are in the process of talking with Mr. Fincham, Tom's partner. I told the police I gave you the address so they may want to discuss that with you."

A police investigator exited the lawyer's office and spotted us.

The secretary immediately pointed to me. "This is the gentlemen to whom I gave Mr. Callas's address."

The investigator shook my hand and asked if he may ask me a few questions. He took us aside, into another room and introduced himself as Inspector Mulder.

Before Mulder could start on a line of questioning, I told him we had already been to see the chief.

"You may want to save yourself some time and talk to him. He has the whole story of our involvement."

The inspector tapped the inter-communication selection on his wrist-comm and waited. After a quick conversation with the chief he nodded at me.

"Thank you. The chief has told you not to leave the city—I suggest you comply with that request."

Mulder left without another word.

"Is Mr. Fincham available to speak to us?" I asked the secretary.

She dabbed at her tearful eyes with a handkerchief, walked along the short hallway and stuck her head into an office. After a second she looked back at us.

"You can come in, Mr. Conroy."

We entered Mr. Fincham's office and sat in the chairs provided. His haggard face told us the story of how his day had started.

"Welcome, Mr. Conroy—Miss Jensen. Forgive my tardiness at making you wait but it's been quite a morning."

I got down to the business at hand and shared the bad news about the loss of my uncle. He seemed a little overwhelmed by the sudden spate of deaths and appeared genuinely upset—we gave him a few moments to recover his composure.

"I'm very concerned about the asteroid mining business my uncle owned. We have a mining project in progress and the staff needs to know what has happened. I have been working with my uncle for the past four months. There has to be some instructions left by him, in the event of his demise."

The lawyer keyed in an instruction on the desk-pad and a holographic file appeared on the viewing platform. He glanced at a few of the entries and then looked at me.

"About four months ago your uncle designated a successor to his business in the event of his death."

I leaned forward with my heart in my mouth.

"That successor is Beckett Conroy, his nephew. Congratulations, Mr. Conroy—you are the sole beneficiary of your uncle's wealth and business."

The air seemed to have been pulled from my lungs. For a few seconds my senses became numb. Carla reached over and placed her hand on mine. "Beckett? Are you okay?"

It took a moment before I could answer in the affirmative.

Fincham gave a wan smile. "I'll prepare the legal documents for the transfer as soon as the coroner supplies me with a valid death certificate. We'll need your digital print as confirmation of your acceptance. It will take a few days."

Carla and I stood to leave. I took her in my arms and said, "Honey, I want to offer you a full-time job."

She laughed. "Only if the pay is better than the EIA's."

We walked out of the lawyer's office arm in arm.

*

Back at the B&B, Freda and my dad sat outside under a tree in the backyard, on a bench. The sunrays radiated through the dome and cast dappled shadows on the ground around the bench.

There were not many gardens around anymore. People did not want to invest time and money on flowers and lawns, but the owner of this place had green thumbs.

My father looked up and smiled as he watched our approach.

"Back from your mission already—how did it go?"

"I'm glad to report it went particularly well, the only downside being we cannot leave town just yet."

"How did the Chief of Police treat you?"

"With respect—he did a double take when we showed him the vial of the Callas murder."

"And did you see Fincham?"

"We did and he showed us Uncle Sid's last will and testament. I am glad to say the Galactic Mineral Mining Corporation has a new owner—me."

My father rose from the bench a little unsteadily while Freda gave support. He took a step forward and placed both arms around my shoulders. It felt so weird but I didn't back down.

"I knew he would do that. Despite his demeanor at the end, he had a good heart. He loved you like a son."

"And yet he came close to killing me, but for Carla."

"Your uncle nursed a grudge against me for years. All my work progressed toward helping the human race to live longer, and he resented that. A year after your mother died he fell into league with a group who were very fundamental in their beliefs and I feared they had brainwashed him—felt I was playing God."

While still in my dad's embrace, the question of my mother came to mind.

"I need to clear one thing up. What really happened before Mom died?"

He fell silent for a few moments and then released me. He needed to look me in the eyes.

"Son—what I'll tell you now is the absolute truth. Your mother and I had a falling out over your Uncle Sid. I know I had treated her badly during my times of extreme project-load. I had become too wrapped up in my work and didn't notice she had started to suffer depression. Your uncle saw the obvious."

I felt a pang of hard-ass but did everything in my power to hear him out.

"Uncle Sid paid her the attention I should have given her. When I found out, the shit hit the fan. He swore they had never got physical, but I felt so hurt—I was torn."

"Go on," I said.

"About that time he bought into the mining project which took him away from Earth for long stretches. Your mother missed him terribly and I felt too angry, too proud, to respond in the way I should have. She ended up taking her life and I have never been the same since."

His dilemma came across to me like a road map to a lost soul. I have never been partial to the deep hurts of others. This had to be a part of my personality many would label as immature selfishness.

My mind reversed the arrow of time to the year I turned fifteen. I remembered some of the family arguments; they would always clam up when asked about their relationship with each other. It confused the hell out of me.

Carla and Freda remained in an uncomfortable silence as dad and I faced off. All of a sudden a wave of capitulation flowed over me. I didn't want to go on with this old fight—my father remained my sole family member. I stepped forward and hugged him.

"It's okay, Dad. We don't need to plow up this old ground anymore. Let's just let it be. Let's allow Mom and Uncle Sid to rest peacefully. We both have new lives to work on."

The words came easily. They represented the most mature things I have said since the day I took off and cut the apron strings. My father smiled and a tear slipped from his eye— the first time I ever saw him cry. We hugged each other in a spirit of forgiveness and a huge weight lifted off my shoulders.

∞∞

Forty-Seven

All's Well that ends Well.

Three weeks later I received a message from the Chief of Police. He cleared me for travel and wished me the best. There would be no case to be brought against the EIA for their activities.

The information had become bogged down with members of the EIA and The Administration but they saw my involvement as incidental. The WGF backed off and left us free from any incrimination with regard to the discovery. They knew nothing about my possession of the information they so dearly sought, or about the resurrection of Padraig Conroy.

Freda and my dad left for Eagle's Nest where his convalescence would continue. He remained keen to resurface after plastic surgery and a new name. Eagle's Nest would become the location of his continued experimentation with consciousness transfer. He vowed to publish a paper on it for the science community once his new identity found an acceptance into the Quantum City regional scientific community.

I decided to go back to the Andromeda and continue the family business of asteroid mining. There would, however, be two new inclusions to the entourage who would accompany me back to the spaceship.

'I have never been into space before, Master Beckett. Will the flight interfere with any of my programming?'

"What nonsense are you pontificating about now, Happydoo?"

The android raised the bionic knuckle to its synthetic mouth and chuckled. *'Good one, Master Beckett, good one.'*

It had only taken three days for Central to supply me with a newly constructed android. Happydoo Two looked exactly as his predecessor and it did much to warm my heart.

Freda and I worked on the old processor, to remove all the details with regard to the discovery and transfer them to a safer place.

There remained one thing I wanted to do. Use the breakthrough on telomere life-extension to benefit the future of mankind. In order to facilitate this I spent two weeks at the New World Earth Institute for more Passive Osmotic Memory Induction on bio-molecular genetics and neuro-science. I also took a memory induction of Business Management Principles in the hope of guiding the asteroid mining business to its fullest potential.

Carla agreed to accompany me. We would get married sometime in the future, once my dad's convalescence was over. There appeared to be a strong potential for the need to carry on the work of longevity. The precariousness of the balance in our solar system and the Earth's failing magnetic field provided the motivation. This remained my father's ardent wish and had his full support.

I turned and looked at my lady-love.

"Are you ready, honey? This will be a new experience for you."

"Ready as I'll ever be," she said.

Happydoo threw in his two credits. *'I hope you are not piloting the craft, Master Beckett. We need someone who is not distracted.'*

I gave him a stern stare and cocked my head in an imitation of the classical android reaction. He immediately broke into the comical, pirouette, foot-stomp routine to express his delight. Things were almost back to normal.

The Excalibur pilot and captain, informed of my uncle's death, waited patiently for us to arrive at the spaceport. The Andromeda staff also eagerly expected us—Carla and I. Their new CEO and his bride to be.

Little did we realize, and just as well, a life's journey of epic proportions awaited us.

∞∞

EPILOGUE

Now you know the extent of my journey, since those first few months aboard the Andromeda. Life has been good to us. Carla now runs our security, a legacy of the knowledge she accumulated with the New World Earth intelligence Agency. Happydoo ended up as my valet and has done a fine job of keeping my affairs in order. My dad and Freda continued to live in the hideaway at Eagle's Nest to follow through on his quest to develop a new identity.

But since the 'consciousness experiment' saga and the early days of my taking the command of Uncle Sid's business, things have gone really awry, as the log will testify:

Andromeda's log.
President Commander, Dr. Beckett Conroy.
18th June, 2367 CE

The Andromeda has suffered severe damage by alien enemy fire. The Crustans are a warlike species from another dimension and have invaded our universe for life support supplies and minerals. We are adrift and without power, protective shields are no longer in operation, weapons will not prime. They will board us soon......

∞∞∞

Pick up on Beckett and Carla's story in the second book of the trilogy:

Survival of a Species: Part Two

The Habitat Relocation Project.